I0659164

Boots

A Novella
of the Civil War

Anthony F. Gero

Camp Pope
2013

Copyright©2013 by Anthony F. Gero

ISBN 978-1-929919-83-3

Library of Congress Control Number: 2013946421

Camp Pope Publishing
P. O. Box 2232
Iowa City, Iowa 52244
www.camppope.com

Cover images: "An Incident of Battle—A Faithful Dog Watching the Dead Body of His Master." *The Soldier in Our Civil War: A Pictorial History of the Conflict, 1861-1865*. New York: Stanley Bradley Publishing Company, 1890. 2:320.
Map of the Battlefield of Gettysburg, Davis George B., et al, *Atlas to Accompany the Official Records of the Civil War*. Washington, DC: US Government Printing Office, 1891-1895. Plate 43.

Acknowledgments:

In any literary work, few authors create in total isolation. Therefore, I wish to acknowledge the efforts of the following persons: to Diane and Phil Windsor for helping to push me at the right time to take a chance, to author Pat Carr who, in her gentle, but firm tutelage, helped a new fiction author emerge and find voice, to Bill Jacobs, always a Marine and faithful Civil War guide, to Clara Silverstein at the Chautauqua Writers' Center for her encouragement, to Clark Kenyon at Camp Pope Publishing whose skills and expertise in the publishing arena were greatly appreciated, to Mary Ann and John Patterson, colleagues in the vineyard of education, to my wife Linda, for her guiding patience and keen observations, to my daughters, Theresa and Katherine, always cheerleading for their dad's writing efforts, and finally to my parents, Lillian and Samuel, a part of the "greatest generation," who instilled in me a work ethic and a drive to take pride in whatever one does; to one and all, heartfelt thanks.

"To be sure, the dog is loyal. But why, on that account, should we take him as an example? He is loyal to men, not to other dogs."

Karl Kraus, Austrian poet

Chapter One

NOVEMBER, 1899—FATHER'S BEDROOM, OWASCO

It was late and I could sense the depth of the night, sitting there in that chair, in that place, in that room with my dying father. I strained to see something familiar through the iced-starred window-panes, but the storm's clouds obscured any hint of the landscape.

"Going to snow," my uncle said as he began to move away from my father's bedside.

"Yep."

Uncle Jack strolled over to the window. He held the curtain aside and peered outside. "All the signs are there."

I nodded.

Uncle tied back the curtains. He gazed out the window for a while longer and then tapped a finger to his lip, turned, and went over to the dog. "Well boyo, I'll see you in the morning."

Boots had raised his head slightly.

Uncle scratched the dog's chin as Boots's tail pounded the floor slowly.

It comforted me to watch this scene of affection.

He rose stiffly and placed a hand on his back to steady himself. He looked down at Boots. "Call me if anything happens."

"I will."

Uncle gave a slight nod, waved, and shut the door behind him. The wind howled fiercely outside. The storm's intensity increased and as I glanced through the window, I saw the large elm tree, just a few rods away from the house. It swayed precariously in the strong gusts. Just a few leaves clung to its dormant branches. It was apparent the wind was picking up and soon even these remaining leaves would be blown away. As a cold surge of wind rumbled through the planking of our farmhouse from the storm's new blasts and chilled me to the core.

Suddenly a voice cried out, "Steady men!"

A new delirium was beginning.

Father's voice was firm as he continued, "Hold!"

Boots barked, but did not rise.

"Wait!" The old company commander's tone was steady. "Wait, I said."

Boots lowered his head, but remained silent.

As we waited, time seemed suspended then father yelled, "Ready on the line!"

Instantly, Boots was up, head tilted, ears flattened.

We both knew what would be said next. The chain of familiar commands we'd experienced in similar episodes over the last few days, as father slipped further away from the present, were starting again. As aspects of his former military life in the Civil War marched into his consciousness and, in vivid detail, played out, his past was alive. For anyone in the room at the time of such a delirium, each had a role to play. Boots and I were ready, again, to play ours.

"Steady boys." Father's voice had a settling calm in its demeanor.

Inevitably, at this point in the delirium, there was a lull. Tonight, as if in response to Father's command, even the strong wind seemed to calm.

Eventually, when the fateful order came, his voice was shrill. "Present!"

Boots bared his teeth and growled, a menacing rumbling reverberating deep in his throat.

"Fire!" Father howled finally.

Boots barked twice in response.

At this point, sweat broke out on my brow and the palms of my hands went cold in anticipation of the next sequence of commands.

"Reload," Father exclaimed. He rose up on his elbows. "Fire at will, give it to them boys! Pour it into them." Then he collapsed on his pillow. From that position in the bed, he spoke in a whisper, "God forgive me."

Chapter Two

LATER THAT NIGHT

I couldn't tell of what battle, of what event, Father's delirious brain had set before him tonight. His present words gave no hint. He had never talked much about the war to me as I grew up. It was as if he had to keep that part of himself hidden in order to protect me from his combat experiences in the Army.

What knowledge I gained about Father's wartime service had mostly come from my visits with my Uncle Jack Hanna, who had served with Father in the 111th New York Volunteer Infantry. Both had volunteered in the summer of 1862 for service in this regiment that was raised from companies recruited in Cayuga and Wayne counties of Central New York.

Uncle Jack and Father had survived countless engagements that the regiment participated in, from Gettysburg through the Wilderness campaign, from the siege at Petersburg through to the end at Appomattox Court House, and I wondered tonight, which one Father's just past delirium had been about.

As I pondered that question, a vivid past memory of my own emerged and placed itself in the forefront of my thoughts. I had been about 7 or 8 and it had been a late summer's day when my uncle sat with me on his front porch. We were enduring a late August heat that comes to Upstate New York and were resting after having picked in my aunt's raspberry bed. She was making some fresh lemonade while my uncle and I stayed out of the way and just talked.

"Sort of reminds me of that day in May, Samuel, when the old 111th New York paraded in the Grand Review in Washington City. We were a true fighting regiment in the Army and well known for our bravery." His head tilted just a bit. "Why even the new president, Mr. Johnson, and General Grant acknowledged that fact by tipping their hats to us as we passed the reviewing stand."

I can still see my uncle's smile.

"Quite an honor that, son, quite an honor."

I had no idea what that presidential salute really meant to my uncle, nor my father since I was too young and naive to understand. That day, I was more concerned about the circus that was in Auburn. We were all going to a matinee performance the next day. Even my father was taking time off from the farm to go to the show with me and that honor colored my reply, " Was it like a circus parade?"

As Uncle rocked slowly in his chair, he could see that my understanding was not clear on what he had said. "No, son, but I've seen the elephant many a time though."

"I saw an elephant once, Uncle Jack."

As he glanced towards me, he had the good sense not to scold my interruption.

"Last year," I continued, "when the circus came to town, Mother got us up very early, just after sunrise and took us to the rail yard. As we got there, we could see the circus train coming and as the engine slowed down, huge clouds of steam rose up!"

Uncle said nothing and just let me continue.

"Behind the engine and coal car, there were all kinds of flat bed

9

cars. Some of them had painted circus wagons on them, and one even held a grand calliope. You could see its bright pipes glowing in the sunlight."

Uncle could probably see the youthful wonder in my face.

"When the train finally stopped, the circus hands jumped off and started to unload. We could just see'em through all the rising steam."

Uncle Jack nodded.

"The animal wagons were unloaded first. As a man with a long hook came by, a ramp was put up on the first car and when the cage door was unlocked, out came an enormous elephant. It must have been 30 hands high." My arms were extended across my body. "While it was led down, the elephant raised its trunk between two huge tusks and trumpeted loudly." With a flourish, my arms dropped. "It was wonderful."

It was then I noticed the small smirk on Uncle Jack's face.

"We all began to clap and shout," I declared, undeterred, "and after a while the circus formed up for the big parade through Auburn with that huge elephant in the lead." As the memory of that morning flashed before me, I paused.

Uncle Jack sensed his opportunity, stopped rocking and began. "I'm sure it was Samuel, but," and with a clearing of his throat continued, "in the War of the Rebellion, that's not what it means really."

"Oh."

He decided to ignore my embarrassment.

"What I meant was that seeing the elephant was our way of saying that we'd been in a real fight during the war." His clay pipe was pointed at me. "It's what we'd say to the new boys, the greenhorns, who'd never been in their first battle." The smoke from his pipe swirled over his head. "Yep, was our way of telling those boys, you really hadn't been in the war till you'd been in a big fight. Yes, sir, a big battle." He nodded. "'Seen the elephant' proper, so to say."

"Was battle just as grand as seeing a real elephant, Uncle Jack?"

His reply came quickly, "No."

"But Miss Jones says the Civil War was the grandest and bravest war America has ever been in."

Uncle eyed me carefully. "Well, I'm not one to contradict your teacher, Samuel, but she's mistaken. There's nothing grand about war."

"Did Father and you see more than one elephant?"

"Many times."

The sadness in his tone was detectable even at my age. Then, as I watched him he put his head back on the chair's headboard as he lifted his eyes towards the sky. It was as if he had now gone away from me. As I grew up, it would not be the first time former veterans, my Father included, would assume that stare when talking about the war. My next question came quickly, "What was the biggest battle you were in Uncle Jack?"

"Gettysburg," he replied quietly, then paused and added, "Your father and I were both there in '63."

Chapter Three

NOVEMBER, 1899—FATHER'S BEDROOM

Perhaps, it was that battle Father's present delirium had returned him to tonight. You couldn't be sure for he'd been in so many, but if I was a betting man, he had relived Gettysburg.

As I continued my vigil tonight, it was then that I noticed that Boots had settled back on his blanket. He was the last in a series of mixed breeds on the farm, all of whom Father called Boots. "Just a mutt, " he would tell anyone who asked about the dog's pedigree. "Nothin' better in the world," and then usually he'd smile. He didn't smile often, but when he did, it was as if a precious gemstone had been unearthed, the brilliance of which warmed all privileged enough to see his smile. In my youth, I had been witness, on occasion, especially in the presence of Boots, to observe that smile's intensity and when it happened, those times had helped me bond with my father and his dog. Looking at this present Boots, I'd have to agree, "Nothin better," I muttered and that sense of familiarity made me feel comfortable.

Father only had one dog at a time on the farm, but each was named Boots. Just why he had kept this tradition was never to told to me by him and since I lacked the courage to ask him why, my chances of finding out the reason he continued to do that had been slim, something I regretted all my life.

My father's lack of explanations of why he did things as I grew up was just not a part of his interaction with me. Although we cared for each other, we could not, or in my case, would not talk much on why he did things. It was if he expected me to accept his orders and directions without question. Maybe it was his experiences as an officer in the war that caused him to be that way, but my inability to relate to his expected acceptance of why and how he did things was, in part, due to my growing adolescent arrogance. There seemed to be this distance between us over why he did things his way, but we didn't hate each other, we just viewed how life was supposed to operate differently.

Once, though, when I was about 14 and thought myself quite stylish, I finally summoned up my growing courage and asked father a question, which had been much on my mind. We were about ready to go to Sunday church services at Westminster Church in Auburn when I saw his white socks, worn with his black suit. At his familiar mode of dress for Sunday worship, which caused me no end of vexation, my long brooding question came blurting out, "Why do you persist in wearing those God awful socks?"

As he reached for his overcoat, he made no reply.

As I came closer to him, I continued my attack. "I mean they're so unfashionable. And they're so embarrassing!"

Father turned, "I didn't know you embarrassed so easily, Samuel?"

As I pressed home my assault, my tone became whiny, "I mean, really, its all the talk among my friends."

His face looked patient as he replied, "So, your friends mean more to you, then, well, I can understand that, son, at your age, but there's more to life than fashion," and with that he turned and continued down the hall way. When he got to the front door, Boots had appeared. Father patted him on the head saying, "Stay."

Boots obeyed.

With a wave of his hand to me, Father shouted, "I'll see Mother and you at church," and was gone without another word.

Frustrated, I turned and went back to the kitchen and saw that Mother was sitting at the large oak table, sipping a cup of tea from her favorite bone china set. It was obvious she'd heard the exchange in the hallway. My tone was not too friendly as I spoke to her, "He's so damn stubborn!"

"He can be," she replied calmly, "at times."

"Those blasted white socks of his make me so mad." My anger was surging. "Why does he wear them?"

She made no comment.

"He should know better than that," I added tartly then stopped my pacing and faced her. "Why doesn't he tell me why he persists in wearing them?"

She decided to answer now. "He doesn't have to explain that to you, Samuel."

"Well," I sputtered, "it makes no sense to me."

As a hint of steam rose above her cup, I could see the rising redness in her face as if she now had decided on something. Her tone, when next she spoke, was stern as she glanced towards a vacant chair. "Sit down."

In our family, when Mother took that tone with you, you did as you were told. With great dignity, she took another sip of tea, then put her cup gently on its saucer. As she looked over at me with a steely cold expression, her voice was soft as she spoke, "It's because of the war, son, he has to wear those white socks. The dye in colored socks causes his feet to get sores. It's something he has had to live with since coming home." Then she stopped and waited to gauge my reaction.

As this new understanding of why Father wore those white socks grew in me, I didn't reply instantly, but when I did, my voice had a hint of regret in it. "But why didn't he tell me that?"

"He doesn't have to, Samuel, he's your father."

I shrugged. "But it's not fair that he didn't tell me that before."

She only tilted her head and gave me a wry smile in response.

My next statement I regretted almost as soon as I uttered it, "Besides, when my friends see him dressed that way, it's so embarrassing!"

She leaned back in her chair. "Well, you'll just have to learn how to handle that embarrassment, Samuel."

I turned away from her, for I could feel my face flushing. "Well," I stammered, "at least I understand his reason for those white socks now, but it still doesn't sit well with me, Mother."

She sighed in exasperation.

"And what of Boots?" I continued. "Why does he call all his dogs by that name?"

She shook her head slowly. "That's to do with the war too," she replied, "and someday, maybe, he'll tell you why, but until then," and she put her hand out, "you'll just have to wait, I'm afraid."

I knew our conversation was about over.

"I know you can do it son," and she patted my hand softly, "you have your father's determination in you and he knows that about you too. Now," she chirped, "let's get ready to go. He's opening today and expects us to be there to greet, properly."

As I rose to go, I was still frowning, something she acknowledged with a slight chuckle. "Men!" It was said with some distain, but no malice in her voice. "Now, lets go, Samuel," she ordered, "Your father is waiting."

As we started to leave, Boots came in as if expecting to join us for the ride into town. "Come on," I chirped as I opened the back door for him, "you can come too."

Chapter Four

1882—My Graduation From Cornell University

After that talk with mother, my acceptance of father's actions in life grew some and it got even better after my leaving home for Cornell University to study engineering.

Father knew some professors there from their Army days together, so my admittance, based upon my academic high school grades, had been accepted.

Once there, joining the Cornell Cadet Corps was predetermined. Although the Corps had become less military and more social by then, the military experiences and camaraderie the Corps gave me an appreciation for a soldier's life, and for that, my father was grateful, and so, in a way, was I too for it helped me to bond with him as well.

Upon my graduation, he came to the Ithaca campus, along with Boots. Mother had died in my sophomore year, a loss Father and I keenly felt, especially on this graduation day, but my older sister Jennifer was there which helped fill in for the loss of my mother.

Doctor Thomas Jones, our local veterinarian and good friend of my father and I attended along with my aunts, Uncle Freemantle, and Uncle Jack. "Won't miss it for the world," Uncle Jack had said to me several times before we had left Auburn.

"Same here," Uncle Freemantle, my Aunt Lillian's husband, would chorus back.

As we all stood on the lawn in front of Barton Hall after the formal ceremony, making small talk, Father finally shook my hand and said, "I'm really proud of you son."

I returned his grand smile with one of my own, saying, "Thank you."

Boots was by Father's side, well groomed and attentive.

It was then that I reached down and patted the dog's head gently, "Glad you're here too, boyo."

He turned, looked up and licked my hand and groaned.

"Good dog," Father said softly," steady now."

As if he was on military parade, Boots obeyed.

"I see," commented Uncle Freemantle at this point, "that you have a job waiting for you in New York City, Samuel."

I turned. "Yes, at the firm of Beardsly, Warn, and Cowan." The pride in my voice was obvious. "My engineering professor sent me down to intern at the firm during several summer vacations and the firm's partners were duly impressed. They told me that, upon graduation, they would offer me a starting position, and so they have." I could see the pride in Father's face as I continued, "As you use to say, Father, 'Success favors the prepared mind.'"

"Indeed," Uncle Jack crooned as he pointed towards the people moving away from where we were standing. "Well, it appears it's time for the reception to begin."

"Quite so," Father replied.

As Boots and I began to move down the walkway with Father towards the dining hall, Aunt Lillian leaned over and whispered in her husband's ear, " A fine looking trio."

"Indeed," Uncle Freemantle replied, "indeed, but Samuel will be missed."

"Yes," and she glanced towards Father, "especially by him."

Eventually, we returned to Auburn so I could get my immediate affairs in order and by early June, Father, Boots, and I were at the train station, huddled on the depot's platform, anxiously waiting for the conductor's final boarding call. We hadn't said much to each other, knowing full well what my job in New York City now meant for us and for our future as a family.

Finally, over the din of travelers' voices and the train's machinery, the conductor sounded, "Board!"

"Have to go now," I said hurriedly.

"Yes, I know, son," and, as we firmly shook hands, that smile of Father's came out. "Good luck to you, Samuel."

At the sound of my name, Boots barked.

My hand went to the dog's face, instinctively, "Good dog."

Boots moaned deeply.

Looking over at Father my comment came quickly, "I'll visit at Thanksgiving."

He nodded. "Yes, to be sure."

Nearby, the conductor was signaling towards the engine, "All aboard!"

The train lurched forward slightly, the ornate passenger cars making high-pitched squeals on the rails.

Grabbing hold of the bar on the nearest coach, I moved to the car's platform steps.

Meanwhile, Father had knelt down next to Boots, and as I watched, he hugged the dog with his left arm and waved with his right.

I returned his salute.

As the train moved forward steadily, clouds of dense swirling steam obscured the two of them from my vision. Suddenly, as if an invisible hand had moved the mists, the gushing vapors separated.

"See you," I called.

I could see Father's mouth moving, but his words were incomprehensible above the din of the train's movements.

Boots was barking, but then his voice too was consumed by the train's acceleration. In an instant, as though that same invisible hand was at work again, the swirling hazes closed around the two of them, and they were lost to me.

While I took my seat, the train gained speed, and we began to move down the line for Elmira where connections to New York City would be made. As the flickering scenery of the countryside sped by my window, the greening spring landscapes held no interest for me. The only scene I could envision was that of Boots and Father on the Auburn platform. The haunting poignancy of them together like that lingered with me all the way to New York City.

Chapter Five

LATE OCTOBER, 1899—A FATEFUL DAY

As my life evolved in that great metropolis, and especially since my marriage to Anne, my travels back to Auburn, to the farm in Owasco, occurred less and less. The necessity of Father's presence there and of my exciting life in the city held us in our respective circles. My work achievements became well documented, something Father noted from the New York City newspaper clippings he kept on me, and which he proudly showed me when I did come home. It was then he got to inspect me, and it was obvious from that look in his eye that he was pleased with my growing maturity and confidence, something that held me in good stead, the day my Uncle Jack's fateful telegram arrived at the firm's office.

I had just gotten to work and noticed the lad in a grey uniform waiting by the clerk's station at the front door. The clerk told me the messenger was for me, so after signing for the telegram, the message's brief meaning was quite clear. I was needed home, immediately, Father was seriously ill.

As my hand knocked loudly on the door of my boss, Mr. Peter Warn, a veteran of the 50th New York Engineers, he replied, "Come in."

As I strode towards his desk, I could see he had a look that told me he had been given word that a telegraph messenger was in the front vestibule. "I've just received this urgent message, sir."

He took the slip of paper, and after glancing at it, looked up calmly. "Your duty lies there, son," then passed the telegram back, "We'll manage here."

"Thank you, sir. I'll cable you as I can."

He pointed toward the door, "Good, Samuel. Now off with you, then."

We shook hands and I left without another word.

Once at my apartment, my overnight bag was hurriedly assembled. Informing my landlady of my unexpected journey was next, and then it was out the front door and into the waiting horse cab. After arriving at Union Station, I purchased a one-way ticket and shortly after, I departed.

Upon reaching Elmira, I found the telegraph office and sent a cable to inform Uncle Jack of my expected arrival time. It was only then that the lack of food and drink became noticeable to me so I purchased some victuals from a restaurateur and found a place in the lobby to wait.

When the northbound train came in, my coffee was half finished and cold. Donut crumbs lay upon my coat, which flew off as I grabbed my bag and rushed to board.

Later as the late train came into the main station at Auburn, Uncle Jack was waiting on the platform. As we embraced, he whispered softly, "Good to have you here, Samuel."

"Father never said a word," I replied.

"No, son, it's not his style." There was a powerful emotion in those words that struck deep. "He didn't want to worry you needlessly."

As we separated, we didn't try to hide the swelling of our emotions, but we said no more, fearful that any further verbal exchange would cause us to lose control of our passions. Once we got through the main doors, we traveled a slight distance to the buggy park. Here we found his single horse rig, got up on it and with my over night bag on my lap, began our journey to the farm.

Once outside of the city, in the fading light of the day, my eyes took in what they could. The hillsides near Owasco Lake were a rusty brown and it was obvious the farmers' harvests had been gathered in. Winter was fast approaching. A slight lake breeze came up now and chilled me and made me huddle closer to my bag. As we made our final approach to the farmhouse, while I peered down the tree lined lane, the lights from inside the house seemed to brighten the pathway and softened the growing darkness, but their shine couldn't lessen my growing apprehension. It was then that I broke the silence we had maintained since leaving Auburn. "Where's Boots?"

"Inside, with your Father," Uncle Jack replied briskly then he lightly touched the horse's rear flank with his whip saying, "almost there."

Chapter Six

At The Farmhouse, Owasco

U pon entering the homestead, Agnes, our long time maid, greeted us in the front hallway. "Good to see you, Mr. Sam."

"Yes, good to see you, too, Agnes."

She took my bag effortlessly, "I'll take that up for you."

Glancing around, I scanned the long corridor. "Where's Boots?"

"Upstairs," her voice was soft as is the custom for speaking in the house of the dying. "The poor soul is with Himself," then she turned and left.

"Here," Uncle Jack said, "let me take your things."

As I gave him my overcoat and bowler hat, he put them on the rack on the wall then ushered me down the main hallway towards the kitchen. All of the important events of the Hanna family took place in that large farm kitchen, and to that familiar place, we were inexorably drawn.

Our progress was heralded by the lusty moans and squawks of the large planked floorboards. The familiarity of those sounds gave me a sense of serenity.

After we entered the kitchen and seated ourselves at the big table across from the open hearth, we waited for Agnes to reappear. In a few moments, she came down the backstairs, saw us by the table and in her gentle Scottish accent addressed us gracefully, "Would you gentlemen care for some tea?"

In a duet worthy of a Gilbert and Sullivan operetta, we chorused, "Yes."

At our unrehearsed display, she smiled broadly.

"And," added Uncle quickly, "are any of those famous molasses cookies of yours left?"

"To be sure," she replied with a hint of mischievousness.

We watched her quietly as she went over to prepare the tea and cookies.

Within a few minutes, the preparation was done so she brought the plate of cookies over, and then fetched the teapot. "There now, that should hold you for a while."

We nodded.

"Thank you, Agnes."

She gave me a quick nod of her head, and then left, for it was quite obvious to her that we now wanted to be alone.

I spoke first, "When did he know?"

"Well," Uncle Jack sighed, "he only told me in July."

I could see the hurt look on my uncle's face that he didn't try to conceal.

"However," he went on, "in talking with Doctor Reid, they may have known about the cancer earlier. June would be my best guess."

"I'd have come sooner."

Uncle reached across the table's top with his right hand. "Your father knew that, but there was nothing to be done." Uncle Jack touched my folded hands, then raised his left hand, palm extended. "Old soldiers, Samuel," and reached for his mug and took a sip. "No need wastin' time on needless rushing about," and put his mug down.

"He knew when the time would be to put out the call to you," and glanced towards me. "No sense signaling in the reserves till now. It was you father's call, Samuel, and he had me send the cable when he thought best."

Usually, Uncle Jack's use of military references tended to irritate me, but not this time. It made good sense, really, to speak this way in reference to what my father had done. He wasn't a professional military man, not a Regular, but the war had greatly influenced him. It had cut notches in him, just as sure as being a farmer had. Life had taught Father how to endure, how not to panic, and I was just beginning to fully understand that. My reply showed my resolve, "I'm glad to be here."

Uncle tilted his head as if he wanted me to say more, so I did.

"Maybe, while I'm here, we'll get a chance to talk some."

"Good," and he thumped the table top for emphasis.

In the meantime, Boots had come down from the upstairs and meandered into the room. He went immediately over to his water dish, lapped from it, and then rambled over towards us.

It was obvious to me that his eyesight was poor and his hearing was suspect and he seemed to be going on instinct. "Here boy!" I cried out, and then as I glanced over towards my uncle, I saw his smirk for it was clear that the old dog was headed in our general direction now.

Boots was close.

"Come on!" I said playfully as I patted my leg for emphasis several times. "Come on, old boy."

Boots seemed to recognize the sound of my voice now and, as his gait increased, he began to wag his tail in a wide arc.

Soon he was close enough to put his head in my lap and it was then that I noticed his grey fur, which showed his age, especially around his mouth. One eye was hazed over with film, but there was a recognition of me that grew the more we touched.

Boots moaned.

It was becoming difficult for me to breathe and tears were filling my eyes as I pressed my face came closer to the dog and said, "Father should have cabled me sooner."

"Steady lad," Uncle Jack counseled. "It wasn't time till now. Besides," he added quickly, "you did answer the call!"

I made no reply to that as I continued to rub Boots face. It was obvious that he was oblivious to what was being said, but it was equally obvious the dog was enjoying my attention.

After a few seconds, my uncle continued on in a most kindly manner. "It's what you father wanted, Samuel."

My head rose and it was then I saw that Uncle Jack's chin was curled up in that way the Hanna's had of showing resolve during times of great difficulty.

"Everything in life is timing, Samuel, when to plant, when to reap, when to fight, and when to die. For every season, there's a time."

"Ecclesiastics?"

"Yes, son, so don't trouble yourself about your father's cancer now."

I responded weakly, "Perhaps."

Uncle's next statement surprised me, "Did you know your father played straight poker quite well in the Army?"

"Really?"

Uncle could see the astonishment in my face. "Yes sir, strange for a Presbyterian too, but he was an accomplished poker player." Uncle chuckled, then cocked his head. "Interesting how life is like straight poker. You can only play what you're dealt, no wild cards, no jokers." Then he paused. "Your father has just one last hand to play, Samuel, and he wanted you here to see it, to be a part of it."

It was then I noticed that several small tears had appeared on my uncle's face.

"He has his reasons, Samuel, so it's good to have you here with him, with us all," and he motioned towards Boots who had his head in my lap still, "real good."

As I looked down towards Boots, his one good eye looked like a pool of deep water. As we held each other's gaze, a flood of calmness washed over me and stilled my troubled heart.

Chapter Seven

November, 1899—Father's Bedroom

Tonight as I sat here nervously in my father's bedroom, I could sense the depth of the night, but I didn't care to examine my pocket watch to know the exact time. My restlessness was countered by the mechanism's steady tick, tick, tick.

My faithful companion's snoring was a diversion. As I looked over toward him, I could see he was curled up tightly in a ball of fur on the old, grey Army blanket Father had saved from the war. "Good to have you here, boyo," I muttered, but just then a sudden cough interrupted me.

The sound came from Father, but judging from this present tremor it was just a minor spasm. Seeing him there in the slim moonlight offered through the frosted windowpanes, he looked like a small piece of flotsam riding the ocean waves. He looked like a mere leaf, just visible in a vast whiteness of flannel sheets, floating between the bed's four columned posters.

That wonderfully carved, maple bed was a family heirloom brought to the Finger Lakes area by my grandfather in 1792. Grandpa Hanna had served in the Pennsylvania Line during the Revolution and had come up to what would become Cayuga County to settle his land grant after the war. His wife, married just before they had left Gettysburg in Adams County, accompanied him. Among the few possessions they placed in the ox-drawn wagon for the trek was this bed.

One of the old traditions they kept in their new frontier home though was the custom of willing this bed to the eldest, surviving child. However, in an egalitarian practice honed from living on the New York frontier, if that child was female, the bed would go to her. Since my sister Jennifer had died more than 3 years ago, a spinster teacher whose fiancé, a captain, a Regular, killed with Custer's main group at the Little Big Horn in 1876 and now buried at Fort Hill Cemetery in Auburn, the bed would pass on to me, as the eldest. As I stared at the bed tonight, the thought of this inheritance made me feel uneasy and caused me to shiver.

In an attempt to purge such unworthy sentiment from my consciousness, my eyes refocused on Boots who still lay at the foot of the bed. His mouth was twitching and his legs moved as if he was running. "Having a dream," I uttered without concerning for speaking aloud.

Boots twitched even more.

Then my mind took over and popped a thought into my head, "What's to become of Boots?" but before my unconscious could reply, a strong shout pierced the air.

"Hold 'em!" Father shrieked.

His loud order caused me to spring, upright, in my chair.

"Steady men," he bellowed as he rose up on his skinny elbows, "Steady!"

His voice sounded fine and strong and I could detect no weakness in it, but another delirium was now beginning. As I gathered up my wits for I sensed a familiar sequence was about to occur like an experienced actor, my lines were already scripted and I just had to wait for my cue.

Boots was up too. His headed was cocked and he appeared alert, poised to respond to his master's orders.

"Wait," Father said just then and dragged the word out, again, slowly, "Wait."

Boots barked twice.

"Steady boy," I whispered, "steady."

He growled aggressively, but didn't bark again.

His deep grumble caused Father to turn and as I watched, he smiled faintly, and then dropped back onto his embroidered pillowcase. His breathing was short and asthmatic and when he spoke, I detected dryness in his tone. "Water."

I rose from my chair and as I approached the bed, on a small nightstand, a green fairy lamp was still lit. Its gentle glow cast enough shimmering light so I could see the glass of water nearby. It was half full.

"Water," he pleaded again.

"Yes, coming," I replied and when near enough, I took the glass with my left hand and raised his head with my right, putting the glass to his parched lips. "Here."

The sounds he made reminded me of ones an animal might make as it lapped water from a dish or a puddle. He never opened his eyes during my ministry and when I finally laid him back on the pillow, all seemed calmer, for the moment.

By that time, Boots had come over and stood next to me. His breaths were labored and his tail was thumping my legs and while I reached down to pat his head, I cooed, "Good boy." At the touch of my hand, he let out a mournful moan. "Now," I said reluctantly, "go over there."

He looked up at me, then turned, and meandered off, dutifully.

When he got to the blanket, he circled it twice, then, as if somebody had set down a large sack of potatoes, he collapsed onto the blanket with a loud thud.

It was obvious to me he wasn't going to last much longer either and so I uttered, "Poor dog." I could feel hot tears swelling in my eyes and standing there, arrogant in the knowledge that I would surely survive Boots and my father, the feeling made me mad. Such is the shame of the living as they watch the old and the dying pass by on their final journey and that shame consumed me as I returned to my chair.

From there, my gaze was drawn back to where father slumbered. Although we hadn't been close in my childhood, yet we had bonded early in life and this link grew stronger once I left home, made my way in the world, and had become my own man. It was remarkable to me just how much he had grown in wisdom after I left for New York City. Such is the intelligence that comes to a son once he is on his own. Soon, I realized, Father would be gone and so would Boots too and I could feel my present despair growing. I had squandered my past times with Father and I wouldn't do so now.

It had become my deduction, later in my life, that father's experiences in the Civil War had made us distant as I grew up. After the war, he had returned home, increased his farm holdings, and continued in the construction of his family's existence, but he could never escape the war's impact. The war had never left him and I had never really understood that about him as I grew up. The gulf between our experiences on how life was to be conducted was never fully bridged until the final illness came for him. I couldn't make up for that lost time between us now, but I could be there at the end for him. That was his desire and mine and it was why he had Uncle Jack cable me and why I had come home.

Just then Boots sighed loud enough for me to hear.

I turned and glanced his way and as my sobs overcame me, my muttering startled even me. "I'll miss you both," then I buried my head in my hands and let my tears flow, without reservation.

Chapter Eight

LATER THAT NIGHT, FATHER'S BEDROOM

It was almost Thanksgiving now and the progress of his cancer had entered the final stages. It was hard for me to see him in this heirloom bed, a mere shell of his former self. Since dying and death are no respecters of the living and treat all men with equality the living do not often extend to their contemporaries, my father's cancer, despite his good name and reputation, consumed him. The acceptance of death's reality was a strain on me, but we were Hannas, a family long schooled in the stoical intimacies of living and dying properly.

I knew he was glad of my companionship these last few weeks, that's why he had allowed the telegraph to be sent. I could tell he was glad to have me there, it showed in his eyes every time I entered this bedroom or when he woke from a nap and saw that I was there.

He had endured so much too since the war. My mother, his wife, Noel, had died giving life to my sister Rachel who had died from an epidemic in New Orleans, which also took her husband and their small son. Rachel had been Father's favorite, but not his favored child.

That child had been my younger brother Robbie who was killed in an accidental event on the farm. A horse had kicked him in the chest while he was in the paddock. The horse, a Percheron, drove a rib into my brother's heart. It was Father who found Robbie slumped on the stable floor.

Father did not have the horse put down, but he did sell the beast since the sight of it, after the funeral, was too much of a reminder. Our friends and neighbors remarked on that, as they had said, "For a farmer, he has too much of a gentle heart."

Now, outside of my two aunts and two uncles who had no surviving children, I was the only direct offspring of the Hanna family in the United States. With the death of my wife, Anne, in the spring of this year, the prospects of the family's continuation were much in doubt.

Yet Father had endured all these events and treated life without bitterness. All he had gone through on the farm, in the war, hadn't changed that. He faced his own death with no bitterness either and his example had taught me a valuable lesson, "Could I do the same?" I wondered when my death comes.

As I grew up he showed me that he was a humble man too, never putting on airs or puffing himself up by vainglorious acts about his military service or accomplishments.

He was a Christian man also, schooled in the belief that life on Earth would continue beyond death. Thus, in his last act of living, he wanted me by his side to witness his passing, to learn one final lesson, to bear, possibly, one last request.

As I reflected on all of these things tonight, a stronger wind gust rattled the bedroom's windowpanes and caused me to look outside. The nearby oak tree was still straining mightily against the wind's force, bending, but not breaking. No snow rushed by, but it was apparent it soon would. As a native Central New Yorker, I had seen such signs before. While I pondered these portents, the fingers of my left hand, in an old habit of mine, went to my lips.

Suddenly, from the direction of father's bed a new series of rumblings occurred.

I turned, and from my quick observations, the heaving of his bed sheets were substantial and his breathing was elevated, so I rose and approached him. When I was within arm's length of him, his right arm flew out and unexpectedly grappled me and drew me in.

"Samuel?" His eyes were slightly open, but he didn't seem to recognize me. His strength amazed me, and when my face was within inches of his, he again exclaimed, "Samuel?"

"Yes, Father it's me."

His eyes were wide open now, the whites around his pupils vivid, but there was a recognition there that I could detect but, in an instant, the delirium took hold. "Do you see 'em coming out of the woods?" and he pointed with his left arm. "There!"

I played my part, "Yes, and they're in line of battle!"

"We've got to hold them."

Just then, as if Nature herself was commanding the opposing forces he saw advancing towards him, the wind responded with a fierce new gust.

Boots had risen, his ears flattened, a deep growl rumbling in his throat.

"Ready on the line," Father screamed.

As if on his command, the wind slackened.

"Wait," he yelled hoarsely. "Wait, I said!"

From past experiences, it was obvious which command would come next.

Finally he screamed, "Fire!"

Boots raised his head and howled lustfully.

The wind, as if in response, gave a surge of energy, the blast of

35

which rattled the windows and shook the walls. In the distance, snow thunder boomed, the echoes of which, like artillery fire, rumbled in the hillsides and rebounded loudly.

The resulting reign of terror made my legs weak. Standing was difficult, but I preserved, and held my ground.

Then, in an instant, Father's present delirium cleared and, as he forced himself to speak, I could see the clarity in his eyes. "Son, remember my dog. Understand?"

"Yes," I stammered, "yes I will."

Instantly, Father's eyes rolled up, then, like a rag doll, his head flopped back, as a rattling gasp issued from his throat. Since the grip of a dying man is strong, I didn't immediately force myself free, but when I finally broke his hold, I placed his head upon the pillow and closed his eyes' lids. As I looked at him now, he seemed asleep.

Boots had come over and had propped himself up, his front paws on the bed, his head next to Father's body. As we leaned into each other, my arms went about the dog's neck. His breaths were strained, but he stayed with me until I felt his strength begin to give way. I grabbed him. "C'mon." I said softly, then cradled him in my arms, and took him back to his blanket. As I put him down, he licked my hand gently, then moaned, curled his head on his hind legs and settled in.

With a final pat, I forced out an emotional "Good boy," rose and left the bedroom for it was now my duty to rouse the household and to alert them to my father's passing.

Chapter Nine

THE NEXT DAY

The next morning, Uncle Jack had left early to fetch Uncle Freemantle and the funeral director. I had dressed, before they left and had come downstairs to wait for them to arrive. Agnes was busy in the kitchen making coffee, the smell of which didn't hearten my mood as it usually did.

Meanwhile, Boots was still upstairs, in my father's room.

As I paced about the parlor, in one of my turns, I looked toward Father's chair. The wooden rocker had been my mother's favorite, and when she died, it had become his. I could still visualize him in it and thought back to about two or three weeks ago, when I had just come inside, having taken Boots for a short walk. Father was sitting there, near the fireplace, alone, bundled up in a checkered blanket. The November cold, which the cancer made him feel more acutely, was fierce that day and I knew, from experience, that the bitter weather hinted at a long winter to come. He looked fragile, but seemed to perk up upon our arrival.

As Boots jogged over to Father, his voice was steady as he greeted me, "So Samuel, how was the walk?"

"Not bad," I replied, "but you can tell a cold season's coming. The air is sharp and the wind is from the northwest." I moved closer to the fire and stretched my hands over the glowing embers. "The clouds are black up towards Weedsport though," I continued as I stared at the fire's small flames, "no telling what's going on there."

"And what's happening with you son," he replied, "now that Annie's been gone these past few months?"

My late wife, Annie, as father called her, had been special for us. She had been Mr. Warn's child, my boss's second daughter, and my father's Godchild and this was the first time since I had gotten home that Father had asked about my life since her death.

I had married late and had lost her to what New York doctors called "city fever" in the spring of this year. It had been a hard blow and, despite Father's present condition, I could tell that his concern for me was genuine. He had come and stayed with me during her final days, but had gone back to Owasco shortly after the funeral. He didn't look right to me when he left, but at the time, I had attributed his condition to the emotions we felt. But now it was apparent that it was his growing cancer that had caused his paleness.

"Work is a distraction," I responded, and then added, "so I manage." It was a stock answer, which I had developed since her death, and I could tell from the expression on his face as I came over to sit by him, that he knew it.

He had been a widower for a long time, and his simple reply was honest, "It's hard," then his voice became filled with a deep passion, "but you'll make do son." He leaned forward and touched my leg. "You always have." As our eyes met, his noteworthy smile appeared.

"Indeed," I whispered back.

He patted my leg several times after that, and then raised his right hand gracefully. "I know you will Samuel, you're a Hanna."

I blushed with pride, but when he saw that, he said nothing about it.

The praise just bestowed was uncommon for him and not lightly given. He expected people to their duty, whether on the farm, in the military, or even just Agnes going about her daily chores. "The Hanna's expect no less," he had sometimes told me as I grew up and he had tried to do his duty all his life. For him to express his pride in me now as he was dying was indeed, a high tribute, yet, as his smile faded, I sensed he was not finished with what he wanted to say, so consequently, I made no comment to his grand gesture.

Boots had risen at this point and had put his head in Father's lap.

As I watched, the old soldier's right hand began to stroke the dog's head, the tenderness of which seemed to me what a lover might bestow on his beloved. Father's present display of emotion was something I hadn't seen for a while and it was good to witness his passion again.

After a fertile pause, he reached over and touched my arm, and then with a slight crack in his voice began to speak with an intensity that surprised me. "It's not good to be alone, Samuel. Not good at all."

Boots turned his head and peered up towards me, his one good eye firmly fixed on me. If the eyes of a dog can look into the soul of a man in a way that no human eyes can do, that dog did it to me now.

In the meanwhile, Father grew quiet and looked longingly into the fire.

My breathing was becoming labored.

Finally father turned and looked out through a large window towards the fields beyond. From where I sat, I could see, just above the ridgeline, that the setting sun was valiantly trying to maintain some light, but could not. Soon the twilight would disappear and give way to a deepening darkness. As the thickening clouds enveloped the heavens, there would be no stars visible tonight.

As I stood there in that parlor the day after his death, looking at that chair, remembering that earlier incident, Agnes's voice called out suddenly, "Coffee's ready, Mr. Sam!"

As I turned to leave, I noticed that Boots was standing in the archway watching me, his tail wagging, ready to accompany me into the kitchen.

Chapter Ten

NOVEMBER, 1899, AUBURN, FATHER'S FUNERAL

The day of my father's funeral started out sunny, but cold. The previous day's storm hadn't fully enveloped our part of Cayuga County, but dark clouds still lingered to the northeast.

"Passed us to the north," Uncle Jack said as we made small talk on the way out of the church. "Up Cato way," then motioned in the general direction of that village, about 14 miles north of Auburn. "Could snow again though," and he looked skyward, "if the wind shifts."

I looked up. "Yep."

My father's funeral ceremony had just concluded and as we exited the crowded sanctuary, the organist ushered us out with an appropriate hymn.

"Careful," I said to my Aunt Caroline who held my arm close for support. "It's slippery on the steps."

"Indeed," then she too glanced skywards quickly, "but the hints are still there for more snow."

I bobbed my head.

After we carefully descended the massive mortared steps, we

moved into the plaza in front of Westminster Church, a beautifully turreted church situated on William Street in Auburn built on land given to the sixty abolitionists who formed the church in 1861. The church itself had been built in 1869, and it was in that year that our family had joined the congregation.

Just across the way from the church, I could make out the Seward house, its yellow painted walls brightly marking the spot where it stood. The Sewards, although Anglicans, attended our church on occasion, especially their son, William Seward, Jr. He had fought bravely in the Civil War in the 9th Heavy Artillery, also raised in Cayuga County, and knew Father from their association during the war.

We were milling around now, anxiously waiting to head up the street towards Fort Hill Cemetery. That place had become the new burial site for the Hannas, ever since the Dutch Reformed Cemetery had closed in Owasco and Fort Hill had opened up. All our past family burials had been moved there and many famous persons were interned at Fort Hill even Secretary of State Seward. Now, it was my father's turn.

As we waited, behind us stood Aunt Lillian and her husband Uncle Freemantle. They were talking quietly. She was showing early signs of dementia, but she knew what was taking place today.

Many family friends, among them Doctor Thomas Jones, were nearby including several local dignitaries.

"I see the former mayor of Auburn, the aged Mr. Wheeler, came," Aunt Caroline whispered softly to me as she waved at him.

"So did Assemblyman Metcalf," I replied. "He must have taken the late train in from Albany, yesterday."

"I'm glad he came, but,'" she snapped, "he was late for the service, this morning."

The sharp edge in her tone made me frown, something she

ignored. Metcalf was from old money in our county and she did not like old moneyed families, nor tardiness, but the Metcalfs were good Republicans and that outweighed the other qualities she didn't like in them.

Just then Congressman John Patterson walked up. "You have my deepest condolences, Samuel." His hand was extended.

"Thank you for coming, Congressman."

"I knew your father from the war. We served together in the Wilderness campaign. He was a good man, a good soldier, and a good Republican." After we finished our handshake, the Congressman tipped his hat towards my Aunt Caroline.

She bowed slightly. "Will you be joining us for the reception afterwards, John?"

"Yes, Caroline, I have no plans to return to Washington, till tomorrow."

She smiled politely and I knew why. As an active suffragette, she never missed an opportunity to engage the Congressman in lobbying for women's suffrage. Not even my father's funeral would prevent her from that, but she would wait till later to do so.

From the look on Patterson's face it was quite obvious he knew it as well.

While the Congressman made his way over to join the rest of the dignitaries, Uncle Jack glanced over towards Caroline and said, "Quite an impressive group."

Doctor Jones had come over at this moment and decided to enter into the conversation, "Yes, all Lincoln men to be sure, Caroline."

"Indeed, gentlemen, all good Republicans," she countered, "just like your father was, Samuel." The hint of steel in her tone was obvious to us all. Amongst the Hannas still living, my aunt was the most political. The fact women still didn't have the right to vote irked her and so she kept pressing on all things political, even here at my father's funeral. "Now, if I can just convince Mr. Patterson," she muttered, "to support the movement for women's suffrage, well wouldn't that be nice!"

As the men about her tried stifle a laugh, the act was not unnoticed by my aunt.

"Men," she sputtered then she decided to keep quiet, for now.

The rest of the mourners were out of the sanctuary too and as they swirled about in bunches at the base of the church's granite steps, they were talking quietly. It was then that former General William Seward, Jr., son of the late Secretary of State William H. Seward, came over. As the commander of Father's Grand Army of the Republic Post, Number 49, The Crocker Post, Seward usually attended a veteran's funeral, but he was not always in residence in Auburn, so to have him here today was an honor. "Samuel, if there's anything I can do, please don't hesitate to call."

"Thank you, General Seward, I will."

He bowed slightly towards my aunts and uncles.

They returned the gesture.

Then Seward spoke loudly, as if he wanted to be heard by those around. "I have always appreciated the Hanna family and what they have stood for in our community and for the nation. Please know that you have my deepest condolences on this sad day," then he bowed again, turned and rejoined the mayor, the congressman, and the other politicos standing off to the side.

"Quite an honor that," Aunt Caroline whispered.

"Indeed," replied Doctor Jones, "indeed. Reminds me of the time he visited our regiment after Cold Harbor in the summer of '64 too."

"A bad place that," Uncle Jack said softly.

"Almost lost General Seward twice that year."

"Indeed Thomas," replied Uncle Jack. "After Cold Harbor, Seward's regiment got sent up to Monocacy in July. Saved Washington City in that battle, that's for sure, but they got whipped doing it. He's a strong man to have on your side though in a fight."

"Now," interrupted Aunt Caroline, "if we can just convince him to support suffrage, too."

But before any of us could reply, some of the veterans of Father's Post were forming up on either side of the steps. They were the honor guard, dressed in fine black suits, with large black crepe armbands tied to their dark woolen overcoats. They stood rigidly to attention, as best as old veterans could, a signal that father's coffin was almost here.

Since the organ music had stopped, I could now detect the pallbearers' steady approach. These local National Guardsmen had been selected to carry the simple rosewood casket on their shoulders since my father's comrades were too old to accomplish the task. The Guardsmen wore their full dress blue uniforms, and as they emerged from the church's entrance, the metal spikes on their black helmets caught the sun's rays. The American flag was still in place on top of the casket, the red, white and blue of the silk cloth adding a dash of brightness to the somber attire of today's ceremony.

As the coffin passed by, the veterans all saluted, while the civilians removed their hats. The only sounds I could hear just then was the tread of the pallbearers down the steps.

Chapter Eleven

OUTSIDE OF WESTMINSTER CHURCH

Out in the street, the black funeral carriage waited. Its matched grey horses were also draped in black and had black plumes on their bridles.

The funeral director's staff, all of which wore black and had black crape tied around their top hats, held the horses in place, but I could see the animal's muscles flexing as they strained in their stance, wanting to move on.

In front of the hearse, the National and GAR Post flags were carried by the Color Guard, all local veterans, one of who was a black man who had served in the 20th United States Colored Troop. Father's Post was not unusual in this since in our area of the state such posts were established, but this was not as common in downstate New York.

The wind was graciously providing a breeze at this point. Over the movements of the pallbearers, the snapping of the silk flags were just audible.

Behind the Color Guard stood a lone drummer, a veteran from the post. His drum was draped in the appropriate black cloth; even his drumsticks were painted black. This venerated drum had been carried home by the 111th in 1865, and upon its front shell the NY shield insignia could be seen, with the regiment's scroll inscribed, "111th New York Volunteers." The drum was now used solely for funeral parades.

At this point, the Right Reverend Philip Windsor joined us, accompanied by Boots. During the service, the dog had been allowed in the church, through the good graces of the Reverend Windsor who had been in the 111th as its chaplain. As he had told me in our meeting to arrange the funeral several day before, "I know the legacy of the original dog intimately Samuel, so this dog's presence during the service is quite proper, in my view."

Consequently, Boots had been allowed to come in with the pallbearers and had stationed himself by the casket. He sat there, erect, never barked, but kept his gaze upon the congregation during the entire service.

Many marveled at the unearthly quality of the dog's performance, my Aunt Caroline among them. Several times I had heard her muttered to her husband, "Oh my, will you look at that." Uncle Jack would then nod, as did Doctor Jones, but they made no reply in response.

Boots, with no word or command either, as if he knew what to do that day, had followed the minister out of the church. Smartly, as if on parade, the dog had come over behind the hearse and stood next to me, his head high, the wind ruffling his fur.

Once the casket was placed inside, the funeral director gave a hand signal to the drummer who then started the cadence. The pallbearers marched on either side of the hearse, in measured step to the drum's sound. Even the horses, it seemed to me, kept stride with the drum's beat that echoed loudly off the surrounding buildings' walls.

Boots moved stiffly forward with me in accordance with the

hearse's movement. I could see that his good eye was alert as he glanced from side to side.

As we continued on, onlookers stood silently as we went by. Men removed their hats, and mothers made their children stand quietly. Many knew whose procession this was, for Father's death notice and wake had garnered much coverage in the local and statewide press.

At the cemetery's main entrance, we came to the large wrought iron gates, which stood wide open. On one side of the archway was situated a small, ornate stone chapel and on the other, a gatehouse. The gatekeeper was there as we passed under the archway, but he stood discreetly to one side, cap in hand, watching us intently.

Chapter Twelve

FORT HILL CEMETERY, AUBURN

Once through the gate's archway, the entourage turned right and went up a small incline following a snow-covered roadway that led to the spot where my mother, brother, and sister were already buried. As we came nearer, I could see the twin poplar trees, which indicated our family's plot.

Nearby, a tall obelisk in the center of several ordered headstones marked the Seward family's plot. The group of gravediggers stood there, discreetly off to the side. They had been able to shovel enough dirt so that Father's remains could be buried and not placed in a hillside vault to await a spring internment.

As the drum cadence ended, the funeral carriage halted. I could hear the horses snorting, whiffs of their vapors rose to mark where they stood in front of the hearse.

As the Color Guard moved off to the side, the pallbearers again took up the casket. As it was carried by, the GAR banner was lowered, but not the American flag.

As Uncle Jack and Boots followed the coffin and the Reverend

Windsor, Doctor Jones had moved closer to help me in assisting my Aunt Caroline to the grave's site.

"Careful," I said,

She glanced at me, "I'll be all right."

"Now, Caroline," said Doctor Jones, "let us help here."

She took his arm too. "Thank you, Thomas."

After the mourners had gathered around the funeral bier, the Reverend Windsor stood at the head of the casket, his plain black gown with white vestments contrasting with the American flag, which still adorned the coffin. He glanced around at this point and when satisfied we were all in place, began to read from his Bible, "As the people of Christ, let us hear the news! The saying is sure and worthy of full acceptance that Jesus came into the world to save sinners. He himself bore our sins in his body on the cross that we might be dead to sin and alive to all that is good. Friends, believe the news and let the people reply, 'In Jesus Christ, we are forgiven'."

And so we responded with "Amen."

It was becoming harder for me to breathe.

"Now, a reading from First Corinthians, Book One. 'Now this I say brethren, that flesh and blood cannot inherit the kingdom of God; neither doth corruption inherit incorruption. Behold, I show you a mystery; we shall not all sleep, but we shall all be changed. In a moment, in the twinkling of an eye, at the last trumpet; for the trumpet shall sound, and the dead shall be raised incorruptible, and we shall change.'"

I glanced towards Doctor Jones and saw his tears.

My aunts and uncle were also moved.

"For this corruptible must put on incorruption," the minister continued, "and this mortal must put on immortality. So when this corruptible shall have put on incorruption, and this mortal shall have put on immortality, then shall be brought to pass the saying that is written, 'Death is swallowed up in victory. O death where is thy sting. O grave where is thy victory,'" and he took a step back from the bier as his final words echoed and seemed to reverberate off the trees.

The pallbearers began to remove the flag, folded it neatly, and then the sergeant in charge walked over and presented the flag to me without any comment, then withdrew.

After that the Reverend Windsor bent over and took up some fresh dirt. "Ashes to ashes, dust to dust, remember Man that thou art dust and to dust thus must return," and threw his handful of dirt on the coffin.

This act was a signal for the rifle squad, stationed a good distance away, to fire their three volleys, the first of which blasted loudly in the cold air. The second volley came quickly, and then a pause, then the third came from their Remington breechloaders. The successive aftershocks caused some nearby tree branches to sway, dropping clumps of snow to the ground.

Soon thereafter, the GAR Post bugler, placed a judicious distance from the grave, sounded "Taps."

As he did, I could see the old veterans raising their arms in a final salute.

Finally, by a long, steady note, which seemed to carry on for quite a time, the lamentable melody ended.

Boots, during all of these rituals, stood next to me, never barking, never flinching.

At this point in the ritual, the funeral director's men reappeared and lowered the casket quickly.

As I watched the coffin's descent, the vastness of the hole loomed large. When the casket was fully lowered, the men pulled up the straps, which reminded me of the whirling of a pinwheel. When they withdrew, the mourners to begin to file by. Some bent down and picked up dirt to toss into the grave, others choose not to.

At this custom, our family watched in grim silence.

Eventually, it was my aunts' and uncles' turn. Uncle Jack came last and, as I looked on, he paused a long time before he took himself away. He went directly to his wife then, arm in arm, they strolled away and never looked back.

Finally, just Doctor Jones, Boots and myself were left.

At that instance, the three gravediggers reappeared, shovels in hand. They worked methodically, and within a quarter of an hour, had finished the job. After they tapped down the freshly mounded earth, they touched their hands to their caps as a sign of respect to us, and moved off.

Instantly, Boots went up to the grave and lay down. His head rested on his front paws, but his one good eye was alert.

As I moved towards the dog, Doctor Jones caught hold of my coat's sleeve and said, "Let him be."

Startled, I turned.

Before I could utter a response, he added, "I'll fetch him later."

The fickled wind, which had been resting for much of the day, blew a sudden strong gust. Its chill cut through our clothing, and instinctively, we turned our overcoats' collars up.

It was then that I noticed that Boots's hair was bristling, but he made no attempt to leave with us.

"He'll find us," Doctor Jones said softly.

"Yes, yes, he will, Doc." I was shivering.

"Let's go, son," then Jones led me away. As we headed back towards the cemetery's front gate, neither of us had the spunk to look back where Boots stood guard. As we journeyed through the open portal, the wind blew stronger, as if to hasten us on our away.

Chapter Thirteen

Later in that same week Boots's lungs had become congested so I had sent for the veterinarian. Doctor Jones had been our farm's vet for years. He had also served with my father in the war, something I knew from talking with Jones on his visits to the farm as I grew up. It was there in the kitchen of our farmhouse, at the end of that fateful week, where he and I were seated. It was early evening. The oil lamps were lit, but a hint of a deep darkness to come was visible through the kitchen's windows over the sink. I knew that tonight would be stark and fiercely black.

Doctor Jones had made Boots the last patient for his day's rounds of farms, and as we sat there, after his examination of the dog was completed, I said, "It was probably that wind which did it."

Jones motioned towards the foot of the stove where Boots lay, "Not much we can do now."

Boots was on an old shag rug.

"It's just a matter of time," he said and shrugged.

Even at that distance, I could detect Boots's hard rasping. "Can you give him some opium for the pain?"

"We can do that," Jones replied as he began to rise from his seat.

As I watched, he headed for his medical bag that sat by the coat rack. He opened the old black leather case; rumbled about, found the syringe and a small glass vial. "Here's the ticket."

"Like two peas in a pod, " I muttered.

"No Samuel, it's more than that." Jones was drawing a measured doze from the vial at this point as he added, "more than that."

As I watched, he finished his task, replaced the vial in his kit bag, and with syringe in hand, headed over toward Boots.

"Never quite understood that about Father and his dogs," I stated rather loudly.

Jones caught the inflection in my tone. "Really." He knelt down, patted Boots gently on his backside, and then injected the opiate into the dog's thigh. "Good boy, that should help."

Boots moaned, but didn't raise his head.

"Care for another cup of tea, Doc?" It was my feeble attempt to get him to stay longer since I had some questions about my father and his various dogs to ask.

"Sounds good. I can use the company, tonight," he replied returning the syringe to his medical kit. He then came back and sat down in a chair opposite me.

By the glance he gave me, I could sense he knew of my desire to talk more so I rose quickly and went to the stove. Taking the copper kettle, I turned and went back towards the sink.

Jones eyed the dog as I worked. "You know," he said in a purely distinctive Central New Yorker's drawl, "Your father really had a kind heart."

Since I detected a hint of mischief in the Doctor's tone I murmured back in a playful way, "Yes, indeed, it sometimes showed itself even to me."

Jones' chuckled. "I'm glad you saw that in your father's

temperament, Samuel. I was wondering if you had noticed that about him."

It was becoming obvious to me that the good doctor was toying with me about my relationship with my father.

As I turned and faced Doctor Jones, he eyed me much as a military scout might, "You know, he was a different man, son, after the war."

Jones's reference to the after effects of the war caused an old rage to take took hold of me. My past anger over what the war had done to my relationship with my father and our ability to communicate erupted "Yes, indeed," I blurted out sarcastically, "it was his defining moment, that's for sure!" I could feel the red hot flush in my face.

Jones chose to ignore my harsh implication and instead he reached inside of his coat and pulled out a cheap, clay pipe. "Do you mind if I have a smoke?"

Since many of the old veterans still used these cheap Army style pipes, another habit they had acquired from their military service, I uttered "No." As I turned back to the sink's water pump's handle, I gave it a vigorous and final thrust. "Go ahead," I called out over the sound of rushing water, "I enjoy the aroma from a good pipe." Then, with kettle in hand, I turned and faced him once again.

If he caught the drift of my new retort, he didn't speak of it. He also hadn't waited for my approval and had already packed some tobacco in the pipe's bowl. He was about to strike up a match, but stopped when he saw my startled expression. "He who hesitates is lost, so they say, son," then lit the match, "such are the lessons one learns in war," and began to draw breath to light the tobacco.

I continued to stare at him.

When he had the mixture going, he withdrew the pipe from his lips. "A smoke can help calm the nerves, we use to say in the Army."

I could only nod in reply.

"Another habit your father and I acquired in the war, Samuel."

It was apparent to me his ploys had been successful for he had been the testing the perimeters of my mood during our verbal skirmish. The old veteran had something he'd decided to tell me concerning the war, my father, and the dogs, but it would be on his terms, not mine. Finally, as I smelled the tobacco's growing aroma, I countered his strategy stating, "Yes, but he didn't talk much about his involvement in the war with me."

As the tobacco's aroma began to permeate the air even more, he could see that I was enjoying the sensation. "A Turkish blend I got used to in the war," he replied. "It's the sandalwood you smell the most, Samuel."

I grinned and proceeded over to a pantry cabinet. Inside I found a cookie tin and preyed off the lid. Immediately, the molasses' scent wafted up and brought back fond memories from my youth in that house.

As he watched me, Jones continued his ploy of disinterest.

I crossed over to a sideboard, got a serving plate and arranged the cookies on it, then went back to the table. With a flourish, I set the feast before him saying, "Voila!"

He surveyed the dish with a quick glance, "Ah, Caroline's famous Joe Frogger cookies."

"Help yourself, Doc!"

He took his pipe and placed it carefully on the tabletop, next to his cup. As he extended his hand, the ugly scar on his right wrist was exposed. The scar started, just behind his shirt's cuff, and extended up his arm. The old wound's surface was ragged and it had had a reddish hue to it that did not match with the rest of his skin's color. He had been wounded at Gettysburg, I knew, and it was there where he had gotten this ugly disfigurement. The sight of that old scar was something I hadn't seen in years. Tonight, it was as if I was seeing it for the first time.

He noticed my uneasiness, but he chose to overlook my discomfort. He had had much practice in people's awkwardness about that old wound and was adept in disregarding their uneasiness upon on seeing it. His tolerance on this was remarkable and was one of the reasons he was highly regarded by the locals and myself.

This virtue of his was counterbalanced, in my view, by his tendency, at times, to pontificate on matters that involved the war. Tonight though, he took no such stance or tone. "Well, this cookie is a real treat, indeed!" and then bit into it, eagerly.

While he was so engaged, I took one too and began to chomp away for my hunger had overcome me as well.

He finished his before I did, but he didn't avail himself of another.

It was then that I saw that mischievous look on his face, again.

"Now that we've eaten, Samuel," and he winked, "let's really talk."

Sprays of cookie crumbs shot from my lips, "Bout what?"

He shook his head and pointed at Boots. "Why, about him!"

As Doctor Jones continued to laugh, I gulped down the last of my cookie and blurted out, "Ok."

"Did your father leave any instruction about the dog, Samuel?"

"No," I stammered as I hurriedly took a gulp of tea.

"Ah, think son," Jones cooed, "did your father mention the dog before he died?"

Gulping down more cold tea, I continued to force myself to relieve the instant of my father's death. Unexpectedly, something reappeared in my consciousness. "Yes, yes, he did," I stammered. "Just before he passed, he told me to, 'Remember my dog.'"

As Jones thumped the table with his right hand, his face broke out in a bright grin. "Right, then. I'll talk to Pastor Windsor, and we can make the arrangements."

I could only stare at Doctor Jones, in disbelief of what he had said.

Jones noted my confusion. "Listen, Samuel, this Boots," and

again pointed towards the dog, "will be buried next to your father at Fort Hill Cemetery."

My incredulity was complete and showed in my reply, "But that's not where the other dogs are buried," I jabbered as my right arm swung towards a back window. "They're buried out back!"

Jones didn't look that way.

"All his dogs are out there!" I exclaimed.

"True enough, Samuel," Jones replied with a chuckle, " a real pet cemetery. Each grave marked with a simple granite head stone, each inscribed with 'Boots,' plus the date of death, but in this case, this last faithful dog is to be buried with full honors next to your father, as was his dying wish."

"Why's this dog so special, Doc?"

As I watched, his smile hadn't abated and he exhaled slightly before going on. "Probably something to do with this one being the last in the line to the first dog."

"Really?"

"Indeed Samuel." Jones's hands were set on the table now. "This Boots is the final direct offspring to that first dog. A mutt to be sure, but a finer lineage in that animal's family tree than many a man in this world can attest to, that's for damn sure." He shared the same attitude with father on the pedigree of his dogs. "A real heart of oak good old Boots is," Doctor Jones exclaimed, then slapped his thigh, "yes, indeed!"

It was apparent now that I would finally find out why. My reply came softly, "Father never did tell me about the first Boots."

Jones gave me a friendly glance and said, "Did you ever ask, son?"

"No."

He shook his head deliberately.

My next reply was just audible, "I'd figured he wouldn't say why."

"We all make mistakes, Samuel." As I glanced towards Doctor

Jones, his hands were raised and open, palms up. "Well now, if you've the time," he replied, his eyes twinkling, "I can fill in some on the first Boots. Isn't that why would asked me to stay?"

"Yes, Doc, thanks, I'd like that very much."

He leaned back in chair, folded his hands behind his head, and became immersed in thought.

By this time, a lump had become so large in my throat that I couldn't say any more, so I waited for him to go on, confident that he would.

Chapter Fourteen

Doctor Jones's Remembrance of Gettysburg

As Doctor Jones prepared himself, I could see a self-assurance building in him.

When he finally began to speak, his tone was firm. "The old regiment, the whole brigade, really," he snorted, "had its pride taken away at Harpers Ferry in 1862. Surrendered, by God," and he thumped the table with his fist, the two white tea mugs jumping slightly, "like a flock of sheep, and told by some damn young staff officer, sent by that blackguard Colonel Miles, to stack our arms and give ourselves up to the Rebs!"

As I watched, Jones's eyes had a fiery fervor in them.

"Never even allowed to fire any shots in our defense, either!" he thundered his words reverberating violently. "Can you believe that?"

I made no rejoinder, since he wasn't really asking me for one. What was obvious was his deep disgust still over what had happened that day when Stonewall Jackson's forces had captured Harpers Ferry.

"The Johnnies were so surprised," Jones continued, "they couldn't believe they'd bagged the whole lot of us so quickly, and at no cost to them in large casualties!"

I knew something of what had happened at that place in 1862, but it wasn't my duty to interrupt Jones with that knowledge. It was his story, and my job was to listen.

"Well now," he continued after a momentary lull, "they couldn't take the whole lot of us with them, just too many of us to guard. Well, sir, before the Reb parole officers showed up at our camp, we stripped our flags from their staffs and hid them, as best we could. Next day, we stacked weapons, and then went in front of their officials, sitting smugly at their field tables to record the rolls of parole. As they sneered at us, we signed our names, raised our right arms, swore to our parole, and were handed a slip of paper. They formed us up, eventually, and marched us off to a nearby field. Thousands of good Union men, disarmed and sent away with a slip of paper, like a white feather of shame, headed towards infamy."

As he paused, I could see his that this memory was starting to get the best of him, for his head was hung low and his hands sat in his lap.

"From a distant rise," he continued, as if talking to the floor, "sitting there on his horse with his whole staff around, General Jackson had witnessed our shame. As we were marched off to that open field, I could see him grinning too."

Jones looked like a defeated man, as he sat there before me.

"They placed us in that field without any tents, their artillery strategically sighted to fire on us, if necessary. Hell, they didn't even feed us, neither," and shook his head. "Well, sir, next day, the 16th of September, 'round 4 A.M.," and his head rose slightly, "we were roused by the guards, formed into companies, and started on the march south. We had to leave our wounded behind since the bastards didn't even provide us with transports. We got to Annapolis on the 24th of September and took ships to Baltimore. When we were got there, we got put on some Baltimore and Ohio trains and transported north to Chicago. Once there, our own government put us in thirty acres of flatland and mud called Camp Douglas!"

The name of that camp was said with great bitterness and, if my interpretation was correct, he had expelled it like a chunk of phlegm, quickly, with extreme force.

"After months in exile at that God awful place," his head was higher at this point as he continued, "we got exchanged for an equal number of Rebs our Army had captured. Was 'round about the end of November then, so we were ordered back to the war and headed east. Our whole brigade, all four regiments, the 125th, the 126th, the 111th, and the 39th, all good New Yorkers, were sent to the Army of the Potomac. Our whole brigade ended up back in Virginia, near Washington City and by the time our regiment got there, there were only about 700 of us fit for service."

As I looked at him, his head was fully up and he seemed to me less angry.

"As we marched by the camps of those other Union soldiers, headed for our new camp, Camp Pomeroy, those veteran boys lined the road side. Some of them started to taunt us." His chin was locked firm, "calling us 'Cowards' and some adding 'Harpers Ferry Cowards' to boot!" His eyes were burning with a fierce intensity, as if he was back on that road, those soldiers' taunts ringing in his ears, the shame of those cat calls alive to his senses.

I could tell from the way he was sitting that he was trying to control himself, but he looked more like a man of war, and there was a pride in his countenance that hadn't been there before.

"Well, sir" he began, "our new brigadier, General Willard, took us in hand soon as we got settled in. Trained our whole brigade earnestly and competently, for he was the first general who saw our worth, who sensed our true fighting spirit, our need for redemption." Jones' face was beaming. "He gave us confidence and nerve, so we trained hard for him. Well sir, in the following days and weeks, we knew that our time would come when we'd be tested in battle. We'd soon see the elephant, that was for sure," and Jones slapped the table hard. "We'd show them all we weren't cowards!" Jones voice was loud. "Take away the white feather that associated with our brigade!"

I moved forward in my seat eagerly.

He noted my movements with a side-glance, and being a good storyteller played to my anticipation skillfully. "Well, Samuel, our time came soon enough. By early June of 1863, rumors were flying that General Lee was on the move, so General Hooker, who was still our commander of the Army of the Potomac, ordered the army to start to head up north. Our whole corps, the famous Second Corps, along with other troops began to move out of their camps. Our cavalry was trying to shadow old Bobby Lee's movements, and they reported back that he had moved out in force towards Pennsylvania." Jones waved his arm casually, "So we proceeded farther up northwards trying to stay along side of him. Lee wanted to invade us again, just like he'd tried in Maryland in 1862, but that invasion ended near Sharpsburg." Jones's voice grew noticeably quieter. "I lost some good friends there."

While he paused, I sipped some tea.

"Well," he continued, "exactly where Lee was going now in '63 wasn't clear though," and Jones looked over at me. "Our regiment was down to eight companies by the time we got up to the border of Maryland by late June and it was becoming apparent that the 2nd Corps was moving into Pennsylvania after that." He was speaking deliberately, as if giving a lecture. "It was early morning of July 2nd and our brigade was on the road from Uniontown. We could tell, even then, that it was going to be another warm day. As the sun got higher in the sky, some of the boys were already suffering from the heat and stragglers were starting to drop out." He raised a finger of his left hand. "Well, sir, as we came nearer to Gettysburg, we could hear the guns firing. We were directed towards Cemetery Ridge and put into a reserve position and ordered to wait. As the day went on, General Sickles moved his entire Corps, the Third Corps, off Cemetery Ridge, down towards Plum Run. Round about 4 P.M, his Corps was in a huge heap of trouble. Just why in the hell old Dan Sickles made that move down off the ridge," and Jones laughed strong enough so that his whole body shook, "without orders from our new Army commander, General Meade, who had replaced Hooker, only God and Sickles know for sure."

I held on to my mug tightly as I waited for Jones to go on.

His right hand was scratching his chin now but in an instant, he stopped. "Sickles had put our whole defensive line in a real pickle and stirred up the Rebs bad. The Third Corps was being pushed back steadily by the enemy and if his men broke," Jones voice became louder, "our whole Army would have been rolled up. Barksdale's Mississippi boys were surging forward round 7 PM. You could see that gray line moving steadily." Jones waved his right arm. "Red battle colors flying and that maddening high pitched yell of theirs." Suddenly, he imitated it, "'Yep, yep, iiee,' they screamed." The old Rebel yell filled the room. "It was as if the whole swale below our position would soon fill with them, moving up to assault Cemetery Ridge." Jones stopped, seemed to deliberate a bit, and then went on. "Well sir, General Hancock, our Second Corps commander was up on the ridge and saw the crisis below in the peach orchard. He turns in his saddle and sees our brigade, four regiments strong, waiting, there. He waves for General Willard to come over.

"'I want you to stop those people from coming forward, General Willard. Plug the hole, knock the hell out of them, but you've got to hurry, man!'

"General Willard looks down into the swale and can see it will be a desperate charge, but he doesn't hesitate. Immediately, he salutes General Hancock, saying 'Sir,' then spurs his horse on before Hancock returns the salute. Willard returns to the brigade and orders the 125th New York and the 126th New York into a line of battle, with the 111th to the left of these two regiments, in reserve. He orders the 39th New York to the extreme left and tells their colonel to guard the flank of the charge from an enemy attack. Once that was done, Willard signals the guidon bearers to move out to help keep the attack formation in line. When that was done, our battle line was formed so he quickly surveys the line and screams, 'Fix Bayonets!'

"The bugles sounded and we snapped those wicked bayonets into place. You could hear the clicking along the line too, like the gears of a clock.

'Right Shoulder Shift, Arms,' the General called out, "And again the bugles sounded! Just like we're on a parade ground exercising the manual of arms, our weapons went up!"

My anticipation was rising as well.

"General Hancock was watching us, the whole time, and I could just make out his smile. Then, with our colors in the middle of each regiment, General Willard orders the advance sounded, and again our bugles played." Jones paused. "As the 125th and 126th headed for God knew what, they passed by General Hancock, who took off his hat in salute, his grin gone, a look of determination on his face."

I could see Jones had a similar look on his face.

"Well, sir, General Willard returned the salute with his sword movement and continued to move forward with his two regiments."

Like Hancock, I felt as if I too was watching this display of military bravado.

"Down that ridge, those two regiments advanced," Jones continued, "a steady line of men."

My heart was beating rapidly.

"On we came, hell bent on redeeming our honor by stopping Barksdale's boys!" Jones was breathing hard. "Well sir, as they moved down into the swale, the Rebel artillery began to shell them right quick. The air was full of deadly metal. Their shots tore gaps in the lines creating horrible holes." The fingers of his left hand stroked his chin "but, despite the terrible losses, the bodies blown apart, the gaps were closed, and our boys pushed on. Into the valley of death they went, a strong line of blue, our General up on his horse. Finally, our buglers and drummers were ordered to sounded the charge!" Jones was pressing forward in his seat, his face flushed. "They broke into a run now, many screaming what was to become our battle cry, 'Remember Harpers Ferry! Remember Harpers Ferry!'"

His voice was shrill, and its harshness chilled me.

'Remember Harpers Ferry!'" he cried again, the old battle cry filling the kitchen.

I cringed.

"It was Armageddon on Plum Run!" he sighed, then firmly places his hands on the top of the table.

My mind raced with battle imagery.

"Those two regiments hit'em hard," he continued in hushed tones, "and it looked like they were slowing the Rebs down, but our Colonel could see that some of Barksdale's Mississippi boys were going to hit the flank of the 126th, so he orders the 111th to charge. Down we came into that swale at the double quick, screaming like devils. We were irresistible." Jones hands were tightly curled. "As we got further into the swale, I saw Barksdale fall, hit several times by our rifle fire, and finally dropped from his saddle. Our men passed over his body and pushed the rest of those Mississippi boys back. As they started to retreat in confusion, soon that whole rocky ground that was threatened to be taken by the enemy was ours!" Doctor Jones turned and the look that he gave me was hard. "Some of the boys pressed on still and only the sounds of our bugles playing 'Recall' stopped them from continuing the charge. We had won that assault, won that ground, and for the moment stood in the relative safety of that swale."

I sensed a note of fear in his tone at this moment.

"It was then, as your father stood next to me, that I looked around, at the ground we had won," and he looked about the kitchen as if it was that rocky swale. "It consisted of scattered boulders, most streaked with blood, as if cans of red paint had been tossed over them haphazardly. Bodies were everywhere, Union and Confederate, even some dead horses lay sprawled around," and he paused, then spoke quietly, "We had won the objective, Samuel, that was for sure, but what was left of the Brigade was in the middle of a slaughter house!" His hands gripped his mug, his knuckles white, and it appeared, too that at any instant he might crush the cup. Suddenly, he got that far away glazed look that veterans sometimes get when they remember their past combat experiences and he just sat there, lost in the past. Finally, he turned and stared at the wall.

From my past dealings with Civil War veterans, it wasn't a good time to interrupt with a sympathetic word, so, as I waited, the only sound I could detect was that of Boots's asthmatic snoring.

Chapter Fifteen

Doctor Jones's Tale Continues

When Jones was finally ready, he turned toward me and began speaking deliberately, "That's when General Willard got killed. He had just given an order to his aide when an enemy shell fragment struck the General in the head, took off part of his face and crown which caused a plume of blood to spray out as he fell. I was standing nearby and caught the body," and Jones stopped a moment before saying, "Almost immediately, another shell burst above too, a fragment of which hit me."

It was then I noticed that he had started to rub his old wrist wound.

"As we fell to the ground," he looked down, "some of the boys rushed over and pulled the General's body off me, then using their rifles as poles, they put him in a sling made from their coats. Another lad grabbed me, then we started back, headed up towards the crest of Cemetery Ridge," and Jones pointed upwards with his left hand. "It still was light enough though to see the carnage that lay about," and he looked away from me, "and I saw many a lad I knew, dead or wounded, among those blades of grass." He curled his lips.

My anticipation was growing over what was to be said next.

"We steadied ourselves though," and he shook his head slightly, "kept to the task at hand, and got back up to our starting point. The whole time, the enemy artillery continued to shell the ridge." He reached out and took a sip of cold tea. "When we passed by General Hancock, I could tell from his look he knew that the boys carried General Willard's body." Jones glanced my way. "Hancock had sent Willard on a death or glory charge, but it was what was needed to be done to make up for Sickles's blunder." Jones paused, "Hancock knew the risks a commander must make, but he was a fighter, always on his horse in battle, always ready to be sacrificed himself if necessary. Got severely wounded for that on the third day at Gettysburg too," Jones smiled. "Hancock refused to dismount at Pickett's Charge. Wanted our men to see him up there on his horse." Jones smacked his lips. "Paid the price for his bravery, just as Willard had. They were those kind of leaders, Samuel, those kind of fighting commanders!"

My mouth felt dry, so I took a sip of cold tea.

Jones turned from me as he continued. "Our party went down the reverse slope," he said, "and occasionally an enemy shell passed over, but none hit us. Finally, we came in sight of our medical station. You could hear the moaning as we approached. When we got closer, we saw piles of legs, feet and arms outside the surgeons' tent. They were still operating as we passed by." It was stated as a mere matter of fact. "The stretchers were lined up with others waiting their turn for the surgeon's saws." Jones voice was firm. "We put the General's body behind one of the tents where the dead were already laid out. After that, they took me to be seen by a medical orderly."

My mind was racing, my frustration taking hold of my thought. "Why hadn't Jones mentioned the first Boots yet? Why all this detail about the second day's fighting? When was he going to tell me about my father?" All these questions darted about in my head, but I had enough good sense left not to say anything. The good Doctor would reveal, in his own time, what he wanted too, but his delay in doing so was maddening.

It was then, with another deep breath, he appeared to steel himself for what was coming next. "We had held the line by that charge of ours, Samuel," began the old doctor, "but our position in that swale was tentative. The survivors of the Third Corps had already started to pull back to the ridge. Our brigade had been ordered to go back up the ridge by General Willard, just before he got killed, but, in some confusion, we still occupied the swale. Well sir, our new commander, Colonel Sherrill ordered, us to pull back, otherwise we'd be isolated. As our survivors withdrew in good order, General Hancock had already reestablished the Army's main line. When the brigade returned, he directed what was left of our gallant outfits be marched off the ridge and placed to the right of the line, near Brian's barn. That was near the center of our main defensive line, and it hadn't yet been attacked in two days, so it seemed a safe place to regroup." Jones's head was shaking. "Little did we know what awaited us there the next day."

I sighed, just loud enough for him to hear my frustration.

He ignored my sigh and continued on, as he wanted. "As night settled in, it was obvious Bobby Lee wasn't finished with us, though." Jones rocked back and forth slightly. "Lee had the bit in his mouth, so to say, and wouldn't let go, but our brigade had redeemed ourselves with that charge, yes sir, took away that white feather of shame, but," like a Shakespearean actor giving a soliloquy, Jones played to his audience, "well, son, on the next day, the third day, our regiment passed into legend."

His words swept over me and, for the moment, my frustration slipped away.

Jones now held a small flask in his hand, and from where he had taken it, I hadn't observed, but it was at his lips as I watched him. He took a quick swig.

I knew that he didn't drink much, especially when making a professional call, but tonight he seemed to need one.

He didn't offer me a dram, but held the flask up and seemed to look at it, lovingly. While he did, it gave me a chance to examine it. It was a bright sliver flask and appeared to have some etched words on it, just below a beautifully engraved American flag motif.

In an instant, he remembered his manners and motioned with the flask at me.

Since it would be impolite not to take a dram, I did so, and got more than I bargained for. As a large measure of that delightful single malt liquor made its way down to my gut, I contorted from the whisky's effects. Jones gave a snort of approval.

Taking the flask back, he held it up, once again, "Present from the boys in the regiment," he said proudly.

My reply was just a quick nod.

Then, without using his spectacles, he pointed to an inscription on the reverse side and began to recite, "To Doctor Thomas Jones, from the men of the iiith New York Volunteers. To the best veterinarian and doctor, ever!" and he laughed most heartily. "Sort of a joke that, really, but an honored one."

The inscription's humor was lost on me, but before I asked as to its true meaning, he had returned the memento to its place. "Well," he exclaimed in a most satisfied way, "here's what I know about the third day at Gettysburg and that first dog called Boots!"

Since my ability to reply was somewhat impaired by the effects of the strong liquor, all I could manage was a short gulp and a quick nod.

He thumped the table for, like a good storyteller, he had set up his audience for this moment. "Didn't forget, Samuel, just wanted to give you an idea of the whole situation first," and he chuckled even more. As he leaned back, he cleared his throat and, in an instant, made ready to transport me to the third day at Gettysburg.

"Now," I thought, excitedly, "now, I'll finally find out about that first dog."

Chapter Sixteen

Doctor Jones's View of Pickett's Charge

"Despite my wound," Doctor Jones began purposefully, "I had returned to the regiment in the late morning of the third day, before the Confederate artillery had begun, since nothing could keep me out of that day's fight. I came back through Ziegler's Grove, and when the lads saw me, some shouted and cried with joy. Some even yelled, 'Ya damned fool,' but I took it in good stead, for the boys were just joking with me."

Several fingers of his left hand were up to his chin and his elbow was on the armrest and he looked quite comfortable, sitting there.

"Pickett's Charge, they call it now in the history books." Jones was taking his time. "Probably 12,000 to 15,000 infantry came out of that tree line, over on Seminary Ridge. It was the afternoon of the third day, and Old Bobby Lee thought he'd end the war right there and then. Wanted to roll his fresh brigades in Pickett's division up that rise, crest over our center, then spread out into our rear. Lee hoped that grand frontal charge would create a panic worse than what had happen to Napoleon's men at Waterloo, where, in the late afternoon, he'd directed his famous Old Guard to charge the British center." Jones had leaned forward and put his hands on the tabletop. "The Brits were positioned upon on the crest of a ridge, like ours, and had been holding on to that position for the previous two days."

I knew enough about Waterloo to understand what Jones was referring to.

"On the French guardsmen came, in their great giant hollow columns, drummers beating their famous cadence. The British pounded them with artillery all the way, but despite the losses, the Old Guard moved up to the crest of that ridge, to see what they could see as the song goes. Well, the British infantry had been ordered to lie down by Wellington during the French artillery barrage so now he ordered them to stand up and open fire." Jones's body jerked as if to mimic the British guardsmen standing up. "Then, in precision blasts by platoons, they blunted the heads of the French columns with a sustained rolling fire. As the smoke cleared, for the first time in the Old Guard's history, they seemed to withdraw," and his voice hesitated. "Well sir, Wellington sees his opportunity and orders the British Brigade of Guards to charge!" The Doctor's voice was rising as he continued, "So with lowered bayonets, they came down the ridge, screaming and yelling like red coated demons."

Jones excitement was growing, as was mine.

"Well, when the rest of the French Army saw the Old Guard pulling back, panic sets in and the French Army began to flee the field and the battle was lost," and Jones turned and looked straight at me. "That's what General Lee wanted us to do at Gettysburg by Pickett's Charge, Samuel. He wanted to panic us, to break the center of our line!"

I nodded.

Jones snorted in reply. "Lee wanted to create a Cannae too, just like Hannibal had done to the Romans in the Punic Wars. That's why Lee ordered General Stuart's cavalry to attack our Army's rear while Pickett hit us in the center on the 3rd day at Gettysburg." Jones snapped his head and smacked his lips, "Almost worked too."

"Go on," I thought, "Go on."

"Well sir, we had General Hunt's cannons up on that line of ours, waiting, not firing much during the enemy's preparatory barrage that came before their infantry attacked. General Hunt was sly, he was setting a trap for those Southern boys, just like Wellington had for the French at Waterloo when he ordered his men to lay down." Like a hunter watching his prey approach, Jones slinked down in his chair. "Our guns lack of fire convinced General Lee that his artillery fire had destroyed most of our guns and so he ordered Pickett's men forward."

Jones' eyes had intensity to them, much like a cat's gaze when sizing up its prey before pouncing.

Quite unexpectedly at this moment, he took an abrupt new approach in his storytelling. "Well, Samuel, even great generals can have a bad day," then winked wickedly toward me, grinning slyly, "on occasion."

As if on cue, the teakettle, which I had forgotten about on the stove, began to whistle and rumble. Its lid seemed ready to pop, so I rushed over.

Jones, rudely interrupted, spoke not a word, but his face showed his anger.

Kettle in hand, I returned quickly to the table. Putting the kettle on an iron trivet, I resumed my chair.

Within seconds, his hard look softened much as the kettle's shimmering had begun to dissipate. "The Rebs opened up their artillery," he started forcefully, "towards about 1 PM. They had over a hundred guns of all calibers firing. Fulmination and smoke, sound and rage, shells flying everywhere, hell bent on destroying as much of our center as possible before their infantry attacked us." He swayed his arms and looked up. "The folks in Harrisburg, over 40 miles away, said later they you could hear the guns, like a thunderstorm, they said." He turned his head back towards me. "Well, Samuel, our regiment was there during that entire barrage, behind a stone wall, near Brian's barn. Although most of the enemy's shells went over us, quite a few fell in our position and we took some hard casualties there, real bad."

I could see the strain on his face.

"The rest of the brigade was there, too, and our new brigade commander, Colonel Sherrill, was hit during the shelling. He was standing with the 39th's Color Guard. Got wounded in the abdomen and died the next day, the 4th of July, ironically."

Jones looked somber now.

"Our regiment seemed an especially favored target for the enemy gunners, too. Several in our Color Guard were killed outright, but others readily took their place and kept the colors flying." He paused, "We lost four color bearers that day holding our position at Brian's barn."

I tried to comprehend the loss of those men holding the flags aloft, wondering why they had stood there so exposed, giving the enemy a point to fire at, but such is the ignorance of civilians as to why soldiers act the way they do in battle.

"Other lads were blown to atoms right before my eyes," his voice was matter of fact. "Why the man next to your father had his head taken off by a solid shot." Jones sighed deeply then added wistfully, "They had just traded places, too."

I gulped as my mind raced with a startling thought. "What if my father had been killed by that barn? If he had, I'd not be here now." I shivered with that realization.

Jones saw my reaction. "Such is luck in combat, Samuel, but mostly the Reb gunners overshot our line. Played havoc with our rear, especially around the field hospital," and he blew a short breath.

"But finally, 'bout 3," and he turned and looked away towards the wall, "their artillery fire slackened. As I watched, like a giant snake, their infantry surged out of the woods. They formed up, as if on dress parade, officers and sergeants dressing the lines. The whole time their massed drummers sounded the 'Long Roll,' which carried quite distinctively across the fields towards our line. I could tell by counting their battle flags," and Jones began to point his finger as if doing just that, "about how many men were preparing to assault us."

I had read about that moment in history books, but now I could envision it too.

"A marvelous sight, Samuel." The awe he had felt that day showed in his tone. He continued, "It's something our lads still talk about to this day," and then he stopped. "Well, son," he went on, "we had a cat's eye view of them and when they finally stepped off to attack us, a gray clad mass of soldiers arrayed in near perfect battle formations, it made you want to cheer those Southern boys, yes sir!"

I could understand why now.

"They moved forward to the sound of their drums, first at a walk, sergeants and officers dressing their lines, with red battle flags waving in the middle of each regiment, guidon bearers out to help keep alignment. On they came, steadily moving up the slight slope. Their skirmishers were in front of the advance, firing on us as they came into rifle range," and Jones turned and looked at me. "We found out later that it was General Davis's Mississippi and North Carolina brigade that was headed towards our position."

I could feel the intensity of the moment in Doctor Jones's eyes.

"Our cannons, which had held their fire during most of the enemy's artillery barrage, began to shell those infantry boys with solid shot at this point. You could see whole lines of men going down, gaps forming, and then filling as they pressed forward. You could see 'em bent over too, hugging their weapons. The air was stirring from our cannons' blasts and it was like those lads were walking into a violent wind storm, struggling to stand upright as they moved toward us."

Jones volume had grown noticeably quieter and it was with difficulty I strained to hear him.

"As they got closer, our guns changed to canister shot and cut more swaths in the enemy's formations! This caused those boys to bunch up," and he pushed his hand together to demonstrate his point. "They seemed to lose their linear formations and were condensing into separate masses and groups, huddled around their flags, but on they came, despite the murderous fire of our cannons!"

I leaned forward.

"Their real target became clearer at this point," and Jones turned and focused his eyes on a point on the wall as he pointed with his left hand. "It was that clump of trees in our line's center. That's where they intended to strike, full force, and thus to overwhelm us by weight of numbers."

He sat back in his chair at this point, and took hold of his mug. "Well," he continued, "we had orders to wait till they were at the Emmitsburg Road, at the rail fence, before we opened up on them. It was easy rifle range, and as the Rebs started to scale the fences, we were ordered to stand up," and he raised his hands. "The command was then passed along. 'Present!' and up went our muskets, rifle hammers pulled back, percussion caps already fitted in place. We could see the Johnnies moving over the fences, trying to reform their lines on the other side. Our Colonel, who stood near our company, screamed, 'Fire!' Then a tremendous volley erupted, followed by huge clouds of smoke and flame which rolled out from our positions."

My senses were tingling.

"The bugles sounded 'Reload,' and like a finely tooled machine, we did so. Within several seconds, the bugles sounded the signal to volley fire and, again, we let loose another blast." His tone was animated. "We were cranking out controlled rifle fire, creating a wall of metal to our front that no human body was ever designed to pass through." He was visibly trembling. "Within seconds, over the din of battle, we heard our bugles sounding "Independent Fire,' so we obeyed," and he paused and put a hand to his face. "Many a brave Southern boy fell out beyond our line, by those fences." As he scratched his cheek, he continued calmly, "Couldn't see too well by that time because of the smoke, but it looked like we stopped them, yes sir, stopped them stone cold." He paused. "How they got that far," he whispered, "was something though."

Without thinking I replied, "Yes, I know."

Instantly, he turned and faced me, his face flushed red. "No, Boy, you don't!"

His eyes pieced me deeply and I could see that the veins on his neck were standing out as if he was ready to pounce, prepared even to harm me, if necessary.

Fortunately, as I sat there, transfixed, I didn't compound my previous blunder with an apology or a gesture or any type of movement.

With a tilt of his head he noted my submissiveness, then, gripping the seat of his chair with both hands, he attempted to control his old battle fury.

While I waited, I had a gut feeling that he was nearing his story's major revelation.

Chapter Seventeen

THE FIRST BOOTS

After several poignant moments, Doctor Jones composed himself, and continued. "Well, Samuel, as I was saying, despite our independent firing, the Rebs still came on up that slope, at least enough of them to worry us. They were quite near now, and although the smoke was heavy, quite unexpectedly, a small breeze kicked up just enough to reveal a sight that made us flinch." As he turned from me, he gestured with his left hand. "Out in front of our position was a cluster of those Johnnies, grouped around their battle flags and in front of them," he tone was striking, "was a brown dog, just a mutt, gamely limping along, a front leg clutched to his side. He kept turning back to those Southern boys, barking loudly, encouraging them to follow him.

"Your father was the first to spot the dog. 'Will you look at that!' he cried out.

"Many of our boys paused which resulted in a lull in our regiment's rate of fire. The Rebs, seeing that, took heart, and one of their officers stepped out front. He waved his arm forward using his sword to point the way, and on they came with a grand yell like fighting gamecocks, their dog still in the lead, barking encouragingly. It was just after that we got the order, passed down the line from officer to officer to, 'Volley fire!'

"Instantly, your father calls out, 'Steady boys! Reload! Take aim on my command!'

"You could hear the lads groan as they went through the loading motions.

"Suddenly, a different voice in our company pleads, 'Not the dog!'

"'Steady there,' counters your father.

"As the boys finished their reloading, I noticed the tears on your father's cheeks.

"In a few seconds, he screams, 'Present!' and up went our weapons.

"Our buglers started to sound the 'Commence Firing,' now and in a few seconds, the whole line erupted in a massive volley as fresh clouds of whitish smoke surged out across those fields. It was then when your Uncle Jack and I heard your father whispering, 'God forgive me.'"

I could see the tears on Doctor Jones's face.

"Suddenly," and he pointed to his right, "that wicked breeze came back and blew strong enough to clear the air and we could just make out mounds of gray heaps, some still twitching on the ground." He was staring straight ahead, fixed on a point on the kitchen's wall. "Clusters of Johnnies, all harvested by our last discharge," and he shook his head slowly. "We had done our duty, had cut down the enemy's last thrust, held the line, but it was a horrible gathering of the sheaves we had gathered in," and Jones paused. "Then, from along our line," he said, "I couldn't say where, a new voice cried, 'Anybody see that mutt?'

"Men strained to look, me among them, but the dog wasn't

visible. As I glanced around, some of our boys were wiping tears away. It was then I saw a big Irishman, Dan O'Shea, leaning on the wall. He was swearing loudly in his thick brogue, 'Damn! Damn! And Goddamn!'

"'Steady there,' your father cries as he put his hand on the big Mick's shoulder.

"'Reload,' the Colonel screams as he moved along the line, 'Fire at will!'"

Jones' breaths were labored as he sat there in our kitchen. It seemed to me that he might not have the strength to go on, but somehow, he found it.

"Well, we kept it up for a few more minutes, till we heard our bugles signaling the 'Cease Fire.' Our men fell exhausted to the ground, their faces caked with black powder, sweat oozing from their clothes." Jones stopped, set his chin firmly in place, and looked down, "and, as the textbooks say, Samuel, 'the rest is history.'"

As I tried to process all Jones had just told me, what impressed me the most was that my father had cried. He rarely cried, it was just not his nature to show much emotion in that way. Some people said it was his Presbyterian upbringing that caused his stoicism; others ascribed it to the reserved nature farmers develop. Regardless of where my father's reticent nature came from, he did cry over that Rebel dog and that fact caused me to have a new appreciation of my father's character.

As I sat there, it seemed to me that Doctor Jones wanted to say more, so after he composed himself, he took a deep breath, cleared his throat, and continued. "The survivors had begun to pull back to their ridge and so we let 'em! Some of the other boys in our Brigade began to jeer at the Johnnies, calling out, 'Fredericksburg, Fredericksburg,' but not the men of the 111th. We took no stock in such jeering," and Jones paused, sighed and then went on. "Unexpectedly, after a few minutes, and without orders, a group of our men went over that wall, your father out in front. I was right behind him. We were looking for that dog. It was O'Shea who found him.

"'Over here,' he shouts.

"As we came closer, we saw that he was on one knee, his massive right hand stroking the dog's matted fur as he crooned, over and over, 'Poor dog!'

I could see the large bloodstains on the dog's fur now.

"Max Schmitt, a former deacon in the Dutch Reformed Church in Owasco, stood nearby. He was sputtering and pointing at the dog, 'Lord, he's the only Christian minded body on either side.'

"'Dig a grave.' It was your father's who gave the order.

"Your Uncle Jack was the first to respond, and then the rest of us drew out our bayonets and started scraping the earth. We got a shallow grave dug, fairly quickly and then O'Shea lifted the dog and tenderly laid the mutt to rest. We covered the site as best we could after which Schmitt marked the place with his bayonet. He put a Confederate cap he found nearby on top and as we stood there, it was then we detected a pitiful moan."

Jones' was trembling.

"'This way,' Charlie Vanderhoff cries out.

"As we moved off to the right, we heard that deep moan again, only closer now. We located the source quickly enough. It was a mortally wounded Reb officer, the same one we had seen waving to his men before our last full volley. He was gut shot and his legs stretched out in front of him, his head on his chest. He was holding his groin with both hands, trying to keep his insides from spilling out."

I tried not to visualize that grim image.

"It was Vanderhoff and you father that were the first there," Jones stated, "and, as they started to lay the wounded man gently on his back, I picked up a discarded knapsack and put it under his head."

Sweat beads had formed on Jones's brow.

"Just as we finished," he continued, "that Reb officer opens his eyes and tries to speak, but his words were faint so your father leaned in closer, as did I.

"'Where's Boots?'

"'Who,' asked your father?

"The Reb draws a breath, best he can, spits some blood, and says, 'Boots, my dog!'

"'Dead,' your father replies and points to his left, 'we just buried him, over there'

"Then doesn't that dying man summon up what little energy he has left and whispers, 'Thanks Yank!'

"Well, Samuel, that Reb rolls his head to the right and tries to motion with it. 'See about his pup, will ya, please.'

"I could see the look of astonishment on your father's face," Jones remarked to me. "Quickly," Jones continued, "your father glanced up and pointed, saying, 'Move!'

"And so I jumped up." As if mimicking what he had done back then, Jones now jerked some. "As I went over that way, I came near a clump of corpses, looking like pins on a bowling green, only thicker in number. It was obvious they had tried to rally round their colors, but their flags were gone. They had already been taken away by some other soldiers from the 126th and sent to the rear as battle trophies." He snorted, "We weren't concerned with such glories."

As the setting sun's glow now backlit him in our kitchen, Doctor Jones looked like a cut out paper silhouette.

"It was then that a small motion in that clump of dead men caught my attention," his hands moved forward as if he was reaching out. "It was a slight movement in one of the dead corporals' jacket. Bending down, I could see the man's uniform move again and, finally, between the gaps in the cloth, between the jacket's buttons, out popped a small, black, fury face. It was a pup, streaked with blood, but alive and only slightly scratched, by the looks of it."

Jones's face glowed now, as if he had seen a miracle that day, at least that was how I interpreted his present expression.

"I carefully pulled the pup up," Jones said reenacting the motion, "and sheltered the dog against my chest. He was shivering. I rose and began to yell, 'He's alive! He's alive!'

"Schimitt hears me, turns and looks over at your father and exclaims, 'It's a miracle!' A real genuine miracle.'

"When I got close, I could see your father's broad smile. Hurriedly, he looks down at the wounded officer and says gently, 'He made it.'

"Well, Samuel, the tenderness in your father's tone was something I'll never forget, no sir, nor would any man who witnessed it."

My heart leapt.

"Well," Jones continued with a flourish of his arm, "I held that pup out, and your father took it and cupped the dog to his breast and bent closer to the Reb. The whole time that dying officer just watched, not saying a word, but I thought I detected a faint smile on his pale lips as your father brings that pup even close to the man's face. Damn if that that Johnnie doesn't murmur, 'Here, boy,' and Lord in heaven, if that pup doesn't yelp with pleasure at the sound of a familiar voice. He starts wiggling his little body and begins to lick that Reb all over his face." Jones was trying hard not to cry.

So was I.

"Well son, that man finally looks your father straight in the face, cause the Reb knew his time was short and says, "Remember my dog!'

"Instantly, your father snaps, 'I will.'

"'Thanks, Yank,' says the dying man.

"Your father turns. 'Here, Thomas!' and passes the pup to me. 'Now, get everybody back to the wall and be quick about it.'

"'Right.' I said, then as we began to move out, I glanced back and saw your father beginning to rise too, but the Reb's left hand went out and grapples on. I couldn't hear what was being said though for the distance was growing between us," and Jones paused.

It was evident he was emotional in his retelling of that incident since I could tell by his facial muscles, which were twitching, making his cheekbones stand out.

"I took our boys back," he continued, "but after I climbed that wall, back to the safety of our lines, the image of your father by that dying man side stayed with me. As I stood there, I could feel the pup's heart beats against my chest. My own beat faster now too as I waited for your father to return." At this point, the good Doctor hesitated in his account, then glanced out the kitchen window, and fell silent.

As I tired to visualize Jones standing there at that wall with that pup, some of my long simmering questions about the first dog had been finally answered. Yet, I had the feeling he still had more to reveal.

Chapter Eighteen

THE NEW PUP

Doctor Jones had started to rub his cheek and in doing so, that ugly scar became quite visible, again to me. When he decided to continue, he began slowly, "With the pup clutched to my chest, I stared out into that field. Your father hadn't appeared yet, and I could still hear sporadic gunfire. I saw others of our men returning with groups of prisoners who had surrendered by the Emmitsburg Road, but the rifle firings off to our left played on my nerves. I was afraid that the enemy might try to reform and advance on us again." Jones stopped and looked squarely towards me. "They were those kind of soldiers, son," then added, softly, "those kind of men."

From what I knew about Lee's troops, Jones's statement seemed appropriate.

"A few moments later," Jones continued, "I spotted your father loping into view. He scaled the wall quickly, breathing hard, and collapsed, his back against the stonework. It was then I noticed that his Army Service Revolver was gone. 'What happened?' I asked.

"He shook his head.

"I decided not to press him on the subject.

"After a few moments, he got up, turned, and gazed intently back into the field. Suddenly, a single pistol shot rang out, its meaning clear to me now." Jones's hands were firmly set upon the kitchen table, and he looked as if he had been mortared in stone. "He never did retrieve that pistol either. Shame too, when you think on it. Was a gift from the Board of Supervisors of the town of Owasco, but now, after that Reb's suicide, it'd be too painful a reminder to have."

I could understand why.

"Well, by now, several of our men had come over to see the pup. Word had spread quickly along our line, and the boys just wanted to look at the dog, to just touch it, to know that something, anything, had been saved from that slaughter in front of us."

Jones was talking softly and it was hard for me to hear him.

"The boys cooed at the pup as they clustered around me, just like a bunch of silly school girls. With powder-blackened hands, they tried to caress the dog too.

"Finally, someone asked, 'What's its name?'

"'Boots!' your father said.

"The men murmured their approval, your Uncle Jack being one too.

"'That's a proper name for him,' declared a lad by the name of Humphreys.'" Then, as if trying to remember his face, Jones face became a mask of concentration.

As I watched, his eyes seemed to look through me, out beyond where I sat. I had seen veterans stare in this manner before and any time I witnessed it, it made me quiver.

"A good boy Humphreys." Jones said finally, the tenor in his voice made me feel uncomfortable, and then his hand thumped the table. "A nice lad too. From an old family who's farm was down towards Moravia. Died in October of '64," the old veteran snorted, "up at Petersburg behind our trench lines at Fort Davis. A sharpshooter killed the lad on a Sunday afternoon, just before sunset. Should've never happened really, but," then Jones stopped and added, "such is war, Samuel, even on the Lord's day."

It was apparent that these remembrances were arduous for the old veteran to recount, but his ability to remember them in such detail, after so many years, was amazing. Tonight, I was grateful he was sharing what had happened that third day at Gettysburg where my father, his men, and that pup had found each other.

Within a few heartbeats, Jones went on. "'Here, Boots,' called another lad as the men continued to jostle about the pup.

"'Here, boy,' said someone else.

"'Let me,' someone new pleaded.

"'Steady there, men,' cries out a familiar voice. It was your father, but there was no joy in his words, 'There'll be plenty of time, later.' He was trying to restore order in the ranks just in case the enemy renewed their assaults on our position."

I could picture my father doing that.

"Yes sir, Samuel, your father knew he had to reestablish control over the men for the day's fighting might not be over. 'Sergeant,' he says to me as he puts a hand on my shoulder, and then slides it down towards the pup. Well, son, doesn't that pup cock its head and commences to lick your father's hand, most heartily. Immediately his smile breaks out and yes sir, in that instant, a permanent bond between a man and a dog was made."

As I watched Doctor Jones at this moment, he looked like a Thomas Nast drawing of Jolly Old St Nick, all red in the face and shaking all over, pipe nearby, with wisps of smoke circling about his head. Jones chuckling was infectious and caused me to chuckle.

"Well, Samuel, the rest of us, we were just uncles to that dog after that. From that day on, that dog was your father's mutt, 'lock, stock and barrel' as they say," and the good doctor paused, then continued.

'Now Thomas,' cries out your father as he slaps me on the back 'get to the rear, you're bleeding again, and take Schmitt here as an escort.'

"I hadn't noticed that my wound had started to seep and had turned my bandage red, but I kept my grip on the pup." Jones was inadvertently stroking his old wound. 'Sir,' says I in my best command voice, then I turned towards Schmitt, 'Let's go.'

"'Back in line men,' your father snaps, and then he turns to your Uncle Jack, 'Skirmishers out!'

"As Schmitt and I left, the men began to respond to the orders. As we made our way back through the grove of trees, headed towards the field hospital, other walking wounded joined us. Some seeing the pup I carried looked at us funny, but Schmitt and I didn't care. Come hell or high water that pup was ours." Without warning, Jones stopped, twisted his lips and drew a deep breath, and just sat there.

Once again, I waited, eager to hear what else he would finally reveal to me.

Chapter Nineteen

The 111th's New Mascot

After this lull in his story telling, much to my growing enlightenment, Doctor Jones resumed his tale. "It rained the whole next day, the 4th of July so the boys still on the line spent it trying to get some shelter and some food. Told me after I returned on the 5th of July that they had been so hungry they had had to rummaged through the haversacks of the dead."

I felt myself thinking that I hoped I'd never be that hungry.

"Next morning," Jones continued, "after I had returned, properly bandaged by a doctor who knew his job, I saw the bodies of some of our dead, a short ways off our firing line. The bodies were put out in a row and most were uncovered. I saw the Whitmore brothers from our company there." Jones stopped abruptly and frowned. "It was a horrible day, Samuel, just horrible!" then he added, "and the smell was just beginning."

Having been raised on a farm, I could appreciate what he had just implied.

"Well, son, our scouts had come back by then and as I was standing next to your father, near the colonel, we could hear the scout leader, a corporal, speaking.

"'They've pulled back, Sir.'

"'How far did you go?'

"'We went all the way to the wood line, the one they came out of on the 3rd.'

"The Colonel peered out across the field with his field glasses," and Jones appeared to look past me. "It was then," he said, "that I noticed the bandage on the Colonel's arm. As he lowered his field glasses, he turned again to the scouts' leader. 'Good job, Corporal.' The Colonel turned and addressed his aide. 'Seems the Rebs have retreated, headed back home for the Old Dominion, Lieutenant.'

"'Indeed, Sir, it appears that way.'

"'Take this message to brigade headquarters. Tell the General, according to our scouting reports, the enemy has pulled back from Seminary Ridge.'

"The aide saluted and left so the Colonel turned towards your father and says, 'When the Lieutenant gets back, Captain Hanna, he'll probably bring word to have our brigade move out to confirm that the enemy has abandoned Seminary Ridge."

"'I agree, Sir.'

"He grunted and looked up and seemed to sniff the air. 'Feels like it's going to rain again,' and then scratches his stubbly chin. 'Well, I'll move down the line now, so keep your men ready. If the order comes, we'll probably be deployed first and I want your company out as skirmishers, Captain Hanna.'

"Your father saluted, but didn't say anything.

"In few moments, the Colonel was out of sight and immediately thereafter your father turns and says to O'Shea, Vanderhoff, Schmitt, and your Uncle Jack, 'We'll move out and find that Reb officer now,' and picks up three shovels which had been leaning against the wall and hands them to the boys. 'You'll stay here, Thomas! I don't want that wound of yours acting up again.' He saw the look of disappointment on my face, but ignored it 'Now,' he said forcefully to the other three men, 'let's move,' whereupon they jumped the wall and went out into the field."

Jones had turned from me and was looking at the kitchen wall again.

"I had left the pup with Chaplain Windsor," Jones said wistfully, "since I knew the dog would be safe with him at the field hospital."

So that's where the Reverend got his connection to the first Boots, I thought.

"It was maybe a quarter of an hour later when the Colonel's aide came back and reported with the message the Colonel had figured on," Jones continued. "Pretty soon our drummers were beating the 'Assembly,' as loud as they could, despite the fact that the previous day's rain had damped their drumheads. It was about then that your father's detail reappeared. When he got inside our lines, he spoke to me quickly, 'Done.'

"'Next to each other?'

"'Yes, Thomas, side by side.'

"It was O'Shea who filled me in on the details now. 'We found the Reb and buried him next to his dog. It was a superficial grave, but the ground was soft enough.'

"'Was the rain,' Vanderhoff blurted out, 'that helped.'

"O'Shea grinned and tilted his head towards Vanderhoff. 'He even made a cross from some ammunition box planks.'

"Vanderhoff nodded, then said, 'and I put the man's cap on it too!'

"It was just then," Jones went on, "that we got the order to fall into line. From there we were ordered to spread out and to move forward as skirmishers. After we were out in the field a ways, the whole regiment followed, arrayed in line of battle as we all headed up toward Seminary Ridge." Doctor Jones stopped again and reached into his coat and pulled out a handkerchief, blew his nose, and then set the cloth on his lap. With both hands on his knees, he looked to me like a flying buttress on a Gothic church. "When we got back from that ridge, we kept that pup with us for the rest of the war too." He sniffed. "Grew into a fine strong dog, but he was your father's dog though, its lord and master, but our men claimed guardianship."

As I took a new sip of tea thinking that some of my questions had been finally answered, I had a feeling that there was more to be told.

"Well," he began, "Boots was with us in every engagement and battle after Gettysburg. Got wounded twice, first time was at the Wilderness. He had gone out with a squad, your Uncle Jack being in charge. They were on picket duty when the enemy tried to sneak up. Why that dog saved those boys from being taken prisoner, otherwise they'd have ended up being sent to Andersonville," then Jones looked squarely at me, "Many a good Union man died and got buried in the rotten clay of that place, Samuel."

I knew of that infamous prison and so nodded accordingly.

"We fought the enemy along that line in Virginia, time after time in '64, since General Grant was that kind of scrapper, but the Wilderness campaign almost did us all in, even General Hancock." The doctor's voice became soft. "It was Ream's Station that almost broke Hancock's heart."

Jones's eyes held a sadness that went to depths I could not comprehend.

"A bad place, the Wilderness, real bad," he muttered, then added a coda, "especially for our regiment at Brock's Road."

I had heard about the Wilderness campaign, of the persistent battles Grant had forced on Lee, of the slaughter at Cold Harbor, but from what I had just heard implied by Jones, that summer and fall of '64 must have been as bad or worse than Gettysburg.

He continued. "We reclaimed our pride at the Bloody Angle, near Spotslvannia Court House, though, and stuck it out along that damned line, till we got the enemy bottled up at Petersburg, near Richmond," and he shook his head. "Then we sat there in those Goddamn trenches for months."

"Damn," I thought. "He's going to go on about that now! When's he going to finish telling me more about that first Boots and his pup?"

Jones saw my look of frustration. "Don't worry, Samuel, I'll not wander anymore," and he smiled, but it looked like a sad smile and said, "Old soldiers son."

I smiled weakly.

"Why Boots was even made an honorary corporal in the regiment. Promoted to that rank by the Colonel after Reams Station." Jones chuckled. "The Colonel had found out about the dog just after Gettysburg, and well, he tolerated the mutt at first, but as the months passed though, he learned to love that dog as much as we did. Why, sometimes Boots would stand next to his horse when we formed up ready to march. Was quite a sight to see, yes sir!" Then Jones's eyes narrowed. "Boots was with us at Ream's Station too when the old 2nd Corps took it bad." He waved his left hand. "We were attacked there by the enemy. They outnumbered us ten to one." He was whispering again. "We weren't the same Corps anymore, too many of the old hands had died and our ranks were filled with new men, so the 2nd broke and ran."

I could see the strain in Jones's face.

"Somehow, though, our line officers and General Hancock rallied the survivors, reformed us, and we finally stood our ground, but we paid a terrible price that day. After the battle, when the roll was called, we saw the butcher's bill. Only three officers, your father being one of them, and 70 men answered the 111th's roll call. Boots was there though, wounded slightly in the thigh trying to help save our colors.

He was standing next to your father at the roll call." Jones stopped, twisted his lips and went on. "O'Shea had been killed in defense of the regiment's flag and Schmitt was taken prisoner." Jones paused, then sighed. "Died at Andersonville." His face was pale. "Well, son, the Colonel looks at your father and sees a tattered remnant of our lost flag in Boots's mouth. 'Damn fine dog, Captain Hanna.'

"'Damn fine, Sir,' your father snaps.

"The Colonel had noticed the dog's wound too. 'Well then, get him to the rear, Captain Hanna!' and then the Colonel added, 'I'll make out the paper for the dog's promotion to the rank of honorary corporal, once we get back to camp.'

"The lads, already despondent over the loss of our flag, disheartened over the poor performance of the old 2nd Corps that day, and keenly feeling the losses of friends at Ream's Station, bucked up at Colonel's statement."

"'Sir,' exclaims your father, and then Boots and he began to move to the rear. As they passed by our thin rank of men, you could see the lads smiling."

Jones had a faint smile on his lips now too.

"The Colonel looks at me, sees my blood smeared face, my bandaged ear, and says loudly, 'Regiment, attention!'

"So, as if we were a full regiment, one thousand strong on the day we marched into Harpers Ferry, what pitiful few of us left tried to come to attention. Some of the boys had to help the nearest man in the ranks, but we obeyed the order, promptly.

"'Shoulder Arms!' the Colonel cries out, then waits. 'Right Face!' he calls and pauses. Finally, he orders, 'Forward, march!'"

The pride in the good Doctor's face was visible to me as he relived that past event now, but the sadness in his eyes was evident too.

After a few moments, he began to speak again, "It took us over a month to recover our regimental strength, but by the beginning of

October, we had over 300 men back on the rolls. Half were drafted men, but some old veterans had returned from leave and hospital as we occupied the lines at Petersburg. Boots had come back too, nicely recovered after the loving care of Chaplain Windsor, but that damn siege at Petersburg went on. It wasn't until April of '65 that we finally flushed General Lee's Army out from behind their defenses." Jones looked at me, "The 2nd Corps helped to do that too!" The glint in his eyes hinted at sweet redemption over what he had implied. "Well, Samuel, we pressed Lee hard that first part of April and cornered him around Appomattox Courthouse. He knew the game was up by then and so he wisely decided to surrender. He was that kind of general, Samuel, didn't want his men to die needlessly for a lost cause," and Jones stopped, smiled at me then turned and looked again towards the kitchen wall.

Chapter Twenty

"Well," he went on, "at the end of April, after having sat on our asses in camp, doing nothing, we got orders to march up to Washington City for a Grand Review, set for May 23rd!" His voice was becoming electric. "It was a beautifully bright day when we passed by the presidential reviewing stand, shoulder to shoulder, what was left of the old hands and the new men, our bayonets flashing, our white gloved hands moving in perfect cadence with the drum beats of our regiment. We were a fine set of veteran soldiers, victors in the war against slavery, proud defenders of the Union!"

His chest was swelling.

"Boots marched right next to your father, at the head of our company. We were just behind our Color Guard, at the front of the regiment. Our massed drums followed us. Step for step that dog matched our measured strides. His fur had been neatly brushed by your father and had a luster that shone. Boots held his head and tail high, as if he knew what this parade was all about." Jones chuckled. "Why, don't ya know, even the new President, Mr. Johnson, stopped his conversation with General Grant on the reviewing stand as we approached. As we passed by, the President tipped his tall black hat to us."

"'Fine set of men,' said the President as he leaned over towards General Grant.

"'And a damn fine dog, too, Mr. President.'

"At least that is what the newspaper reporters who were standing nearby said they heard those two men say. The next day, word of that exchange was all over the Northern papers. The boys were well pleased to read about it, and many a copy of those papers were bought and kept as souvenirs. Mine hangs, framed, on the wall in my bedroom."

Jones smiled and his infectious grin had caught hold of me as well.

"Well, Samuel," he continued, "after the parade, when we finally got sent back to Auburn, there was a grand parade here. It started from the train station and went down to the Western Exchange Hotel on Genesee Street, right through the center of town."

I knew of that hotel. General Lafayette of Revolutionary War fame had visited in 1824 and had stayed there. It was there where all Auburn's important events ended up.

"Boots was out in front again as we marched up to the Western Exchange. Many in the crowd noted his fine showing and his steady pace, too." Jones' voice rose. "Why they even hung a huge banner across the street, 'Welcome Victorious Conquerors,' it said in bold gold letters." He was on the edge of his seat. "As we stood in formation in front of the hotel, Boots was next to your father. The mayor, our state assemblyman, our state senator, even our congressman were on the hotel's balcony. Well, sir, the bell in City Hall was being rung and after twelve tolls, it stopped and the crowd roared their approval lustfully. I can still hear it." He raised his chin. "Why it was a grand day, son, just grand." Jones glanced over at me and winked.

I gave him a wry smile in return.

"After some speeches by the dignitaries," he went on, "the town fed us. Had to open up every hotel in the city to do it. Why even Boots was allowed in and he ate quite well, as I remember it. Well now, two days later we were formally mustered out, and former Corporal Boots took to his new home in Owasco real well. He was often seen with your father in that buggy of his when he came to town. The old dog even sired a pup or two after he got used to his new surroundings," and Jones cast a sly glance towards where Boots lay. "Hail to the conquering hero," the Doctor said as he raised his mug, "and hail to his offspring too."

Boots didn't stir at this salute since the opium had worked quite well.

"Like withered leaves," Jones muttered then his voice grew faint. "Just the way of it, Samuel" then lowered his mug and pointed at the dog, "Soon he'll be gone too." Jones twisted in his chair and looked at me. "Old Boots there is the last of the direct line from that first dog, son, far as I know."

"So that's why father called each of his dogs Boots."

"Yes. It helps to keep alive the memory of those brave Rebs and that loyal dog of theirs too." Jones had some fresh tears streaking down his face and he didn't try to wipe them away. "Your father did what had to be done up by the Brian barn that day at Gettysburg, but finding that pup gave him, gave all of us in the regiment, a sense of hope, of possible renewal." A queer look appeared on the good doctor's face as he continued, "Here we were enemies, bent on killing and maiming the other then, suddenly, that pup gives us common ground. Odd, isn't it."

"No," I replied softly, "not at all."

"Well," he said, "that's my take on the whole story of those first dogs, Samuel. I wish you father could have told you, but he could rarely bring himself to talk about that day at Gettysburg and what it meant to him, or us." Jones looked back towards the present Boots. "Life goes on as they say," and with a deep sigh, he composed himself, rose stiffly, and strode over to the dog.

Boots didn't stir at all upon the Doctor's approach.

He bent down. "Good old dog."

The old dog's tail thumped slowly, once, then twice, then stopped as the Doctor finally withdrew his hand.

"I'm glad I came home, Doc."

He turned. His broad smile had reappeared, but he didn't say anything.

I was up, my hand extended. "Thanks, you've been a real help tonight."

He crossed over and took my hand, firmly. "It's good to have you home Samuel." After we separated, the old soldier squared his shoulders. "Your father would be proud."

I bowed slightly, but made no reply for my emotions were welling up.

Doctor Jones strode purposefully to the coat rack, grabbed his overcoat and put it over his arm. He then bent down, picked up his medical kit, turned and called out, "Goodnight."

"Good night, Doc."

Just before he left, he glanced poignantly toward the old dog, but said nothing. It was the last time Doctor Jones saw Boots alive.

Chapter Twenty-one

The next day, as the first rays of the early morning light flashed in bright streaks over the barren hills near our farmhouse, radiant beams shone through my bedroom windows. It was as if a hundred candles had been lit to announce the day's start, so I rose. My sleep had been fitful for most of the night as my mind wouldn't settle itself and, immediately, I noticed that Boots was not at the end of the bed, on that old Army blanket I had moved from my father's room to mine. Consequently, I rushed down the back stairs and found the dog by the foot of the kitchen stove. His breathing was heavy and sounded painful. I bent down and touched him saying, "There you are."

He moaned pitifully.

"Good boy," and then I sat down beside him.

His eyes opened, ever so slightly and he raised his head and put it in my lap. His tail began to pound rhythmically on the floor.

I could feel my hot tears welling up, blurring my vision.

Finally, after a few more seconds, Boots closed his eyes and, with a long deep breath, was gone.

As the sun's brilliance continued to brighten that room, I pulled him closer, my sobs uncontrollable. Finally, I laid him back on his blanket. He looked peaceful. I rose, turned away, and went, reluctantly, up the back stairs to my room to dress.

We held the dog's funeral several days later in the Memorial Chapel, near the main entrance of Westminster Church. The chapel had been dedicated in 1876, during the Centennial of the nation's founding, to those church members who had served and died in the Civil War. The modest chamber sat about 40 people in a beautifully designed, intimate space. Finely carved latticework lined the white washed walls and two tastefully crafted stained glass windows, designed by Tiffany and Company from New York City, flanked the communion table up front. Upon that simple counter, a large plain wooden cross stood. On either side of it, two pure white candles, in unpretentious pewter candleholders had been arranged. As we filed in, as was the tradition in our church, the candles were not lit.

The chapel felt comfortable, like an intimate sitting room, and held none of the vastness of the main church, at least in my view. Many others in the congregation felt as I did, and that was why I had asked the minister to conduct the dog's service there. My Uncle Jack and I had met prior to today's service with the Reverend Windsor in his private study, in the main church building, to discuss my request to hold the service in the chapel. Windsor had immediately put us at ease. "I'd be honored, Samuel to perform the ceremony, despite what some might think. Those dogs of your father, especially this last one, meant a lot to him and to us, as veterans of the 111th."

"Indeed they did," added my uncle quickly.

"Thank you Reverend Windsor," I answered. "And can we use my father's flag for the coffin?"

"Quite so!" the minister said as he gave me a quick nod. "Have you picked out some hymns yet?"

I gave him a slip of paper of the song selections I had written on it.

He read it quickly and said, "I'll have the church secretary order up some printed bulletins. Here's the Scripture reading" and he passed me a slip of paper. "Will you be so kind as to read the Old Testament liturgy?"

I looked at the passage and verse numbers written down and said, "I'd be honored, sir."

"Good! I'll see you on Friday, Samuel, say around 9:00 AM. We'll start at 10, so we can discuss any last minute arrangements just prior to that."

"Yes," I replied as we shook hands cordially, whereupon my uncle and I departed.

On that Friday, the day of the service, members of father's GAR Post, as many as could attend, especially the veterans of the 111th, were present. Once again, as at my father's funeral, upon their black coats were arrayed their war medals. Large black armbands were on their coat sleeves and all wore white, Berlin style gloves, since not to do so would be improper, especially in honor of the deceased.

My family members were in the front pews, the ones usually reserved for the family of the deceased. As I glanced nervously around, the rest of the mourners had filed in quietly. The stark contrasts of colors in their dress to the colors in the chapel were vivid and made quite an impression on me. It was the same sensation I had had at my father's funeral and it was that feeling now that made me feel comfortable, again. Doctor Jones sat beside me and it was to him I spoke, "Quite a display," I mumbled

"Yes," he replied, "yes, it is."

My aunts and Uncle Jack sat behind me, but I noticed, as I glanced backwards, that Uncle Freemantle was not there. "Is he going to be late, today?" I asked Uncle Jack.

"No, Samuel, he's at home, bedridden with a cold."

"Is it bad?"

"It's pneumonia," the implication being quite clear. "Got it at the funeral, I'm afraid, but he's sent a note," and passed it to me.

I opened it.

"Dear Samuel,

Regrettably, I cannot come today so offer, instead, these few lines in humble condolence. Words are always inadequate at times such as this, but they are the best we can do.

Please know that I knew of the first Boots too and have always shared a love for that dog and his descendants that your father and the men of his regiment had. I deeply appreciate that you came home, at the end, to be with him and his dog. They are together now in death, as in life, in peaceful slumber at Fort Hill.

One day, they will be waiting to greet us on the other side, so, until then,

I remain, your loving and faithful uncle,

Robert Freemantle."

As I slumped forward, note in hand, Doctor Jones put his arm around my shoulder. On the verge of tears, I looked up at the small, plain coffin of pine already positioned at the communion table's base. Draped over the casket was the same flag that had adorned my father's coffin, its bright colors adding a dash of luster in the muted chapel's surroundings. The pallbearers had positioned the cloth so it wouldn't touch the floor, as it would be inappropriate for the flag to be so displayed.

I had informed Doctor Jones previously of my wish to use my father's flag for Boots's coffin and the good Doctor's reply was typical for him. "It's a grand gesture, Samuel, grand. I don't believe any in the Post will object either."

One last detail of today's service stood upon the communion table. It was a small bouquet of dried straw flowers Aunt Caroline had insisted be placed there, in front of the cross in memory of Boots and Father. As I looked at those flowers now, she saw me staring and so leaned over and said. "They both loved flowers so."

"Yes they did," I replied.

She smiled and was about to say something more, but a small commotion at the back of the chapel indicated that the minister was there and ready to start.

Chapter Twenty-two

THE FUNERAL

The service was to be a simple one since no animal's funeral had ever been conducted in this church before. As the Reverend Windsor entered the chapel with a young boy acolyte, they went quickly up the center aisle. When they got to the communion table, the lad lit the two candles, turned, and withdrew.

While that occurred, the minister stood behind the lectern and surveyed the chapel, then raised his hands saying, "Please stand and join with me in the call to worship for today."

Within seconds, as the congregation rose, the chapel was filled with the sounds of bodies in motion.

"Bless our God, all people," he exclaimed.

"Let the sound of God's praise be heard," we responded in tandem as we read from the printed bulletins.

"God has kept us among the living," he continued.

"And has not let our feet slip," we replied.

"Bless be God who has not rejected our prayer."

"Or removed God's steadfast love from us."

"Please join with me," said the Reverend Windsor, "in singing Hymn 263, 'Immortal, Invisible, God Only Wise'."

Since there was no organ in the chapel, we sang without accompaniment. Doctor Jones took the lead; his baritone voice began in a low pitch that set the tone for our singing. Since many in attendance were men, the harmonies of that particular hymn were quite deep and moving for me. All the verses were sung, even if the hymn had six of them. Presbyterians were known for this custom, and for Boots's service that convention was rigidly maintained.

As the last of the hymn's words concluded, the minister spoke loudly, "If we say we have no sin, we deceive ourselves, and the truth is not in us. But if we confess our sins, God who is faithful and just will forgive us our sins and cleanse us from all unrighteousness. In humility and faith, let us confess to God our sins."

"Gracious God," we replied, "our sins are too heavy to carry and too deep to undo. Forgive what our lips tremble to name and what our hearts can no longer bear. Set us free from a past that we cannot change; open to us a future in which we can be changed; through Jesus Christ, Amen."

As the last word echoed, the minister said, "Please be seated."

And we did.

"The Old Scripture reading will be by Mr. Samuel Hanna," then the minister stepped back and took his seat behind the podium.

I rose, went to the lectern and fingered the appropriate page of the Bible that lay open before me. "A reading from Ecclesiastes." I could hear my voice reverberate in the room. "Chapter 4, verses 2-12." As a few coughs greeted my statement, they were finished quickly, but in that lull that followed, a growing silence became deafening, so I drew a deep breath and continued. "Wherefore I praised the dead which are already dead more than the living which are yet alive.

"Yea, better is he than both they, which hath not yet been, who hath not seen the evil work that is done under the sun. Again, I considered all travails, and every right work, that for this a man is envied of his neighbour. This is also vanity and vexation of spirit.

"The fool foldeth his hands together, and eateth his own flesh.

"Better is an handful with quietness, than both the hands full with travail and vexation of spirit." I paused. My eyes were tearing, but I took a new breath, girded my loins, and went on.

"Then I returned, and I saw vanity under the sun.

"There is one alone, and there is not a second; yea, he hath neither child nor brother; yet is there no end of all his labour; neither is his eye satisfied with riches; neither saith he, For who do I labour, and bereave my soul of good? This is also vanity, yea, it is a sore travail."

I glanced up and noticed that Doctor Jones was wiping his right eye with a handkerchief. Others were doing the same, Uncle Jack unashamedly so.

"Two are better than one;" I went on "because they have a good reward for their labour.

"For if they fall, the one will lift up his fellow; but woe to him that is alone when he falleth; for he hath not another to help him up.

"Again, if two lie together, then they have heat; but how can one be warm alone?

"And if one prevails against him, two shall withstand him; and a threefold cord is not quickly broken. The Word of the Lord."

And the congregation chorused back strongly, "Thanks be to God"

After I went back to my pew, Doctor Jones whispered, "Good job, Samuel."

I nodded and tried to keep in control of my growing emotions. The Reverend Windsor returned to the lectern and gripped its sides. I could see the effort he was making to control his emotions by the color of his knuckles that were turning white. Just then, some rays of light shone through the stained glass windows, as he started to speak, "Good friends, there will be no homily since none is needed for this faithful dog." He looked towards the coffin. "We all know about the legacy of this dog, and of his family's grand lineage, so, instead of a homily about the deceased, since we are all God's creatures, let us instead, stand as one and join together in saying the Lord's Prayer."

We did so with conviction. Finally, we chorused the "Amen" and after that, Uncle Jack leaned over the pew and passed his handkerchief to me. It was already quite moist, but I didn't care.

"Now," the minister called out, "as our recessional song, please turn in your hymnal and let us sing 'Amazing Grace'."

And so we did.

As the final verse began, "When we've been there ten thousand years," the Reverend Windsor began to move to the back of the chapel. He was half way down the aisle at, "bright shining as the sun, we're no less day to sing God's praise," and by the conclusion, "Then when we'd first begun," he stood in the archway. From there he started his benediction in a strong, clear voice. "Now, go out into the world and hold on to what is good. Return no one evil for evil and strengthen the faint hearted." His voice rose. "Honor all men, trusting in God's goodness and mercy. And let the people of God say, Amen," and we did.

Immediately, the two pallbearers, members of the GAR Post who had volunteered and who were healthy enough to carry the coffin, rose from their front pew and moved to the casket which they hoisted on their shoulders. As they began to move down the center aisle, their hats were off, held in their opposite side hands. The reverberations their shuffling made was in greater proportion to what it was and their movements seemed to fill the chapel's chambers.

Our family followed out behind the casket exiting, as was the custom, from the front of the chapel. Everyone else was still standing as we passed by and it was evident that many were manfully trying to control their emotions.

Chapter Twenty-three

AT THE GRAVESITE

Once out in the street, our small funeral procession made its way towards the cemetery. It had begun to snow, gently, the large flakes floating gracefully down. Some that landed on my face felt quite moist and blended with my tears.

The streets were almost absent of people, but those who were still out and about looked at our small procession curiously; their faces drawn with concern and some confusion. From their viewpoint, I surmised, the size of the coffin suggested a child's funeral, but the GAR veterans in the procession, plus the Post bugler, made no sense for a child's funeral. Neither did the flag draped on the coffin. We made no attempt to inform them of who it was that was carried in our entourage, for it would not have been appropriate to do so just then.

Finally, we arrived at the gravesite, where, at the foot of Father's plot, a small funeral bier waited. Boots's casket was placed on it, and then the flag was removed, folded precisely, and handed back to me without a word spoken.

As the snowflakes settled on his balding head, neither did the

Reverend Windsor speak, nor read from his bible as he waited, placidly.

During these activities, the mourners watched silently too.

Finally, the two gravediggers appeared and lowered the coffin expertly, which was the signal for the Post's bugler. As he began to moisten his lips to play "Taps," we could hear him spitting into his mouthpiece. When the mournful tune began, the old soldiers snapped to attention and saluted.

I placed my hand over my heart while my aunts did the same.

Eventually, the last bugle note sounded, the bugler making sure it was a long sustained note, which was a signal for the mourners to begin to file by. First the Reverend Windsor threw a handful of dirt into the grave, and then the others did the same. No one chose not to follow this custom. As these handfuls of earth struck the casket, their impact had a distinctive finality to the ceremony.

Uncle Jack was last to come by. He stood at the open grave for a long moment and then tossed a silver dollar in.

Doctor Jones, who stood next to me, saw the look of confusion on my face, so he leaned in and whispered, "An old Army custom that."

I turned to him. "Really?"

"For the entrance fee to Fiddler's Green, Samuel."

"Ah, I know of that place. Father sometimes would take me to his GAR Post meetings and the old vets would sing of Fiddler's Green."

Jones grinned and tapped my arm. "Indeed, an old Army song."

Finally, as we watched him, Uncle Jack saluted and left to join his wife. As they walked away, he never looked back at us, or at the open grave.

Presently, only Doctor Jones, the two gravediggers, and I were left.

I looked at them, nodded, and they began to do their job working in tandem while I watched them without uttering a word. So did Doctor Jones.

It took only a few minutes before the grave was filled in, and the dirt tapped down. The diggers glanced our way, tipped their fingers to their workmen caps, then left, shovels resting on their shoulders.

The snowfall had increased and big soft flakes covered our shoulders like a shawl. We could feel the heavy moisture in the snow, its dampness chilling us, but we were indifferent to it by now. Some flakes had layered themselves on our bowler hats too for a newly developed storm had arrived and was enveloping everything around.

Quite unexpectedly, Jones took a brass marker from his overcoat pocket, and then held it out so I could read it. "To Boots," it read, "a true heart of oak." Jones saw my smile, returned it with one of his own, then moved towards the grave.

As I watched, he bent over and carefully placed the marker on Boots's grave. Next, he rose, surveyed its placement, and then just stood there. Within a few seconds, the snow made short work of blurring Boots's fine new plaque so Doctor Jones knelt down this time and, with his white-gloved right hand, made broad strokes to brush away the fresh snow. Within a few seconds, however, his efforts were made futile, so he rose again, stood to attention, and saluted.

When he finally turned away, I had just about lowered my right hand from over my heart.

He nodded, approvingly.

Then, in concert, we withdrew. By the time we had almost reached the cemetery's main entrance, the snowfall had shrouded the entire confines of Fort Hill Cemetery. It was as if a thick blanket of pristine white had been spread over the grounds. Even the trees, mostly pine trees, were layered with snow as if decorated for the coming holidays.

"Quite beautiful," Doctor Jones said as he glanced around, then looked sideways at me. "Quite marvelous."

"Yes."

He caught my halfhearted tone, but his reply came confidently, "It's the invisible hand of God that's created this winter wonderland today, Samuel." My blank expression caused him to frown and then to shake his head slowly. "Even in the midst of grief," he whispered, "God can show us that he is with us."

I could think of no adequate reply to his statement of faith, for I was now adrift in my sorrows.

Jones put his arm around my shoulder and so we continued from where my father rested in sweet slumber with Boots by his side.

We were almost to the gate's archway when Jones spoke again. "Remember, Samuel, go to sleep in peace, for God is on watch."

I tried to grin, but could not. When we passed through the archway, the gatekeeper was nowhere to be seen.

The wind had quieted, but it was still snowing, steadily. All around us, a peaceful silence lingered and was our companion as we headed to Westminster Church where our carriage waited to take us home.

Chapter Twenty-four

Early Morning, Owasco

It was three days later after that storm, a rare Nor'easter, had ended, and I was still in residence at our farm. I had already wired Mr. Warn in New York City to request leave to remain through the New Year, and he had wired back that, "Since business in New York is slow, STOP! It is quite acceptable to extend through the New Year, STOP! As always, W. STOP"' Frugal as ever, I reflected, but at least he understands my need to be home for a while longer.

This morning, on what was to be my transformation, I had been in the kitchen preparing a meager breakfast of coffee and cold fruited scones. Agnes had requested leave to be with her kin in Syracuse for Christmas saying, "It's my sister's birthday, Mr. Sam."

"Yes Agnes, fear not, I can manage."

"I can leave you some meat pies that you can warm up though."

"Thank you."

"And there's scones I can whip up that should tide you over, sir, till I get back."

"I'll be all right, Agnes, now off with you, and a Happy Christmas to you all."

"Thank you, Mr. Sam and the same to you, sir."

She left the next day and caught the intercity trolley to Syracuse, having baked all the previous day to stock up. I hadn't eaten the pies yet, however, since her day old scones and some fresh brewed coffee would, I thought this morning, "Do me just fine."

As I busied myself, dressed in my black velvet bathrobe and red slippers, the front door bells sounded. My coffee had just begun to perk so, taking the pot off the burner; I headed towards the front hallway. As I shuffled along, the bells rang again and this second ringing irked me. "Well," I sputtered then called out, "I'm coming!"

My fumbling with the front door keys taken down from the vestibule key rack didn't help my mood. As I hurried to open the inside door, then the outside one, the bells rang again. Finally the outside door opened, just enough for me to say, "Yes?"

Surprisingly, nobody was visible in my line of sight since our porch was a step down from the door's threshold and the emptiness before me was startling. Who could be playing such a trick this early, I wondered?

A distinct muffled noise caught my attention so I looked down. Then, to my surprise before me appeared a young boy. My quick assessment was that he was about 5 or 6 years of age. He was fully clothed in a heavy multicolored overcoat and oversized black boots. He wore a blue knitted woolen hat with earflaps tied down under his chin. As a further defense against the raw December wind, he also wore a red woolen face scarf, wrapped around his head, and stretched over his mouth. Above that two bright blue eyes were visible. His nose protruded over the scarf and his skin tone seemed to match the scarf in color. Swirling vapors rose from his nose and partially shrouded the rest of his face. In his gloved hands, he held a medium size wicker basket who's top was closed and tied shut by a string latch and wooden block.

As I gazed dumfounded, the boy spoke, "Mr. Hanna?"

As a result of this, his scarf moved and disclosed more of his features. His cheeks were ruby red and a bright smile was spreading across his facial contours. As he looked up, one front tooth was missing too! At such a cherubic sight, I could feel my gruffness ebbing. "That's right."

Instantly, as high as he could, he held up the basket. "My Paw said I was to give you this."

"Well, thank you!" As I clutched the offered gift, a sharp gust of wind blew across our porch and made me clutch my robe closer around my neck. "Now, who might you be?"

"I'm Billy Vanderhoff!"

I detected gleefulness in his tone, which indicated that he was quite proud of his ability to recite his name.

"Oh," then I paused and struggled to recall that family's name.

While I was so preoccupied, the young lad began to rock slowly on his heels.

As I pondered who his family was, the cold seemed to cut deeper into me, then, suddenly, it came to me, "I knew them." They were members of our family's church and lived nearly three miles away. Their grandfather, Earl Vanderhoff, had enlisted in the 111th and had served as a corporal in my father's company. Earl had survived Gettysburg, but had been severely wounded during the Wilderness Campaign and eventually sent to a hospital in Rochester. He was discharged, came back to Owasco, and had often visited our farm during my childhood. I had made Mr. Vanderhoff's acquaintance on those visits and, like my father, Mr. Vanderhoff had not talked much to me about the war, but he was always glad to see me and especially Boots. Then I remembered too what Doctor Jones had recently told me about Vanderhoff being there when they had found that Reb officer, his dog, and that pup. All these facts seemed to come together at this moment so I blurted, "Yes, Billy, I knew your grandfather!"

But, before I could say more, the child produced an envelope. "Here. I was told to give you this, too!"

Shifting the basket to my left arm, I was about to reply when the boy turned and suddenly dashed off. I could hear his laughter as he bounded down the steps and ran towards a painted red sleigh, which stood in the lane, just off the front gate. Upon reaching his transport, he hopped in the front seat and covered himself with a blanket.

It was then that the driver turned and waved.

I waved back as best I could with my free hand, the unopened envelope acting like a fan.

The driver saw my salute, and then flicked his long whip. I could see the effects on the horse that immediately pranced forward, snow scattering about as it struggled to pull the load. Within a few strides, the animal had achieved a steady pace and the sleigh seemed to glide effortlessly across the newly crusted snow.

As if on cue, the sharp westerly wind faded.

Instantly, my ears caught the crisp jingling of sleigh bells. I hadn't heard these particular melodic chimes since my youth. Such chimes, if used in New York City, were often lost in the clamor of that metropolis's street noises and so this present sleigh's bells melody brought back fond memories. As I stood there on the porch, quite unexpectedly, a new sound came and interrupted my nostalgia. I looked at the basket. "Whimpers?" I murmured, then immediately rushed inside, forgetting to lock either door in my haste.

I went directly over to the marbled topped side table that stood in the front hallway, as a series of tinny whines began which, after I carefully set the basket down, stopped. My curiosity was only heightened when, after a few seconds, a new series of whimpers came from inside the basket, then ceased.

Without thinking, I giggled and as my head rose, it was then that I noticed my reflection in the gilded mirror above the side table. My hair had been tousled and my cheeks were flushed, a ruddy red. My robe's velvet collar was still pulled up and, if I was not so excited now to look inside the basket, I might have roared with laughter at my disheveled appearance, but, just then, a series of whines caused me to look down.

Chapter Twenty-five

A NEW BEGINNING

Carefully, I opened the basket's cover and what appeared before me was a plain bright blue cloth blanket that undulated and bobbed, rising and falling like rolling ocean waves. The blanket seemed to have a life of its own.

"Now that's interesting," I casually said out loud.

As the folds separated, a small, brown dog's face appeared. As the pup's two enormous black eyes looked up, the animal seemed to take my measure.

"Well, there," I crooned and let the pup smell the back of my left hand.

The animal sniffed it, then licked my hand most heartily, but in an instant, stopped abruptly and began to pant, a sure sign of nervousness.

"Good boy." My tone was calm, but firm since I had been brought up by my father in the knowledge of how to handle strange dogs. I could feel myself smiling as I said, "You're okay."

With a tilt of his head, the pup eyed me again, and then licked my hand, near the wrist this time.

Taking that as a sign of acceptance with both hands, I lifted him up and drew him close. "There, there, now, you're safe here."

He let me hold him without struggling, his tiny hind legs dangling, his head back, tongue extended. From my quick inspection, I could tell he was a male dog too. His eyes appeared to glow and had a friendliness in them, an unspoken warmth of acceptance, which, as we gazed at each other, seemed mutual.

My heart leapt.

It was at this point I decided to sit down in the cushioned chair off to the table's side. As I made a lap for the pup, he looked around, decided it was safe, and began to settle in, but I did keep one hand on his back, just in case he tried to leap from my lap.

We stayed that way for a while as I stroked him gently, then I remembered the unread note, which had been stuffed hastily into my robe's pocket. With one hand continuing to steady the pup, and with the other inside my robe's pocket, I began to fumble around.

These motions stirred the pup.

"There now, it'll be all right." It was my voice's tenor that helped to calm him, not the words I had said, another trick I had learned from my father in handling animals.

The pup decided it was still safe, and so quit his squirming.

When I finally got hold of the note, I held it up and noticed the envelope's plain white front cover. Upon it was written, in bold black strokes, a formal greeting, " To Samuel Hanna, Esquire." The envelope was not sealed, just tucked in so the note's removal was accomplished fairly easily, but it did take two hands to achieve that task.

The pup was glancing about during this movement, but he made no attempt to leap from my lap, but he began to squirm.

I could feel his twitching on my legs though and said, "Be good, now." As I shot him a quick side-glance, he settled back, reluctantly, but it wouldn't be long before he tried to get away. Such is the pent-up energy of pups, the knowledge of which I had acquired on our farm.

With my time limited, I unfolded the message rapidly. It was written on a fine quality paper, probably used for special occasions was my hunch. The cursive penmanship showed an elegant grace, and this is what it said:

"Dear Mr. Hanna,

Herein you will find a pup that we hope you will most kindly accept. We know that this dog cannot replace the loss of Boots, nor of your father, but we trust that you will find a place for this dog in your house, as another breathe of life.

We remain,

Most cordially and respectfully,

Lydia, Benjamin, Sarah, William, and Betty Vanderhoff."

Underneath those names, signed separately in a descending list, was each individual's signature. The first two were craftily written and showed an adult's firmness.

The third signature was cruder. "A youth's," was my thought.

The last two signatures had letters that had been formed in a wavy script, as if someone had held a small hand to help the writer in the completion of the signature. My chuckling came spontaneously as did a single uttered word, "Remarkable."

The pup drew back his head and yelped once, defensively.

"There, didn't mean to frighten you."

He looked around tentatively, raised his head a little, then decided it was still safe enough, so settled back into my lap. I did notice though that his ears were up and pointed forward. The hair on the back of his neck was upright, too, all of which indicated to me my time was running short for him to stay any longer with me in that chair. As a result, I put the note on the tabletop, rose and shifted the dog onto my right arm. With the pup nestled there, we moved down the hallway towards the kitchen.

"How about something to eat?"

The pup cocked its head, panted, then turned and raised his eyes towards me.

There was a gleam there, which caused me to giggle like I had as a child on Christmas morning.

"C'mon," I cried encouragingly.

The dog had shifted its position; its front two paws now extended beyond the crux of my arm. It seemed that he was quite comfortable in his high perch and it appeared to me that he was getting use to my presence.

As the threshold of the kitchen entrance got closer, I felt a growing warm glow inside of me. "Now, what will I call you?"

The pup seemed to ignore my question. Its mouth was open, its small tongue extended, but it appeared not to be afraid since its ears were not raised.

I could sense his rapid and strong heartbeat against my chest too and as we passed through the rounded archway, the idea came to me in a twinkling and my words burst out. "What about Boots!"

The pup perked up, yelped once, then once more.

"Boots, it is!" I cried out blissfully as my chest swelled with emotion.

Just then a brilliant spread of light from the sun's rays came through the window over the sink. Their yellow glow, as if an invisible hand had directed a spotlight into this place, illuminated the room and appeared to search out every shadowed corner.

As the pup turned his head towards me, his tiny pink tongue had flopped to the side. He looked quite comical, which made me chuckle and, in that joyful moment, it was as if my father's spirit surged through me. My heart, which had been heavy with sorrow, was lifted. My transformation was made for the meaning of those dogs, of the men who had loved them, had finally been stamped on my soul. Now, I wouldn't be alone either.

"C'mon," I cried out excitedly as I put the pup down, "let's see what we can find to eat." Going towards the food pantry, I didn't need to glance back for I knew Boots was following close behind.

www.ingramcontent.com/pod-product-compliance
Lightning Source LLC
Chambersburg PA
CBHW050802250626
47155CB00005B/2175